The Ultimate Surrender

The Ultimate Surrender

A Cavallo Brothers Romance

Elsa Winckler

TULE
PUBLISHING

Chapter One

Two years ago

S HE COULDN'T HELP it, she had to do it. The photographer was late, she had her makeup on, her hair was ready, so she could indulge before she had to work.

Lifting her face up to the sun, drinking in the fragrance that was the Seychelles, Hannah lifted the layers of pink tulle of the skirt she was wearing and twirled. Sandy, the makeup artist and the hair stylist laughed.

"I was wondering when you'd do that," Sandy said. Looking over her shoulder, Sandy grinned. "Looks like our photographer caught you in the act."

Hannah looked up into a pair of dark brown eyes that were watching her over the lens of a camera. This had to be Darryn Cavallo. The rumors were true—he was drop-dead gorgeous. Tall, muscled, with tousled, ink-black hair. Wow.

She didn't wait to be introduced to him, didn't wait to listen to his instructions. With her eyes locked on him, she slid into a pose. He stared at her for another minute before he lifted the camera.

And then her body started moving to a beat only audible

to her and the photographer. Without any conscious thought, she posed and turned, instinctively knowing exactly what he wanted her to do.

The air around her stopped moving, breathing became difficult, any minute now she was going to go up in flames. Every cell in her body was reacting to him.

As a model, she was used to being looked at through a camera lens, used to the bold stares of photographers wanting to capture the perfect moment, but never before had anyone's stare lit a fire inside of her.

She'd been modeling professionally for a year now and this was the first time her path had crossed with Darryn Cavallo's. But she'd heard about him ever since her first shoot. Apart from the fact that everyone talked about how attractive he was, he was considered the best fashion photographer in the business.

The fact he was here, willing to do this shoot with her, had her agent in raptures for days. Hannah hadn't been able to understand the fuss. Yes, his photographs all had that mystical "extra" nobody could really define, but there were other good photographers as well.

And then she'd looked up just now to find his eyes taking in everything about her.

There was something in his stare that melted her bones, put her heartbeat into overdrive, and boiled her blood. In about ten seconds flat, she had tumbled into love, lust, or something. For the first time in her life, she understood what her romance-writing mother referred to in her many stories.

They were on a private beach, necessary for the second part of the day's shoot. For the next few shots she would only be wearing a bikini bottom. She'd be lying on the sand, so her breasts would be covered, but even after all this time, taking off her top in front of a whole crew of people was still not an easy thing to do. And now, Darryn would be looking as well.

The thought excited her already over-stimulated body. How was she to survive the next hour or so wearing next to nothing while this man was looking at her, his eyes fixed on her?

The sun was hovering on the horizon, and they only had a few minutes of daylight for these particular shots. The makeup artist and hair stylist hurried her into the nearby tent so she could change.

Her palms were sweaty, and her hands trembled as she slipped out of the skirt and top. Slipping the bikini bottom on, she looked into the mirror and nearly groaned out loud.

"Are you cold, sweetie?" the hair stylist asked and handed her a toweling gown to slip on.

"A little," she said, biting back a sound. She had to try and get her body under control before the shoot.

A few minutes later, she walked back, taking deep breaths.

"Okay, everyone!" Darryn didn't shout; he merely raised his voice and everyone listened.

"I want everyone gone. It's just going to be me and Hannah. I'll signal you when we've finished."

Hannah. So he knew her name.

Everyone stared at him. This was very unusual.

"Scoot," he said and, lifting his camera, walked closer to her.

Hesitantly, his assistant followed him.

"You too, Rick," Darryn said without looking behind him, and with one last frown in their direction, the assistant followed the rest of the crew from the beach.

Darryn put his camera down and walked over to where she was standing.

"Hannah," he said, and her heart tripped.

His gaze dropped, he clenched his jaw, and when he looked up, she knew he'd seen her body's reaction to him. His eyes darkened.

Mesmerized, she licked her suddenly dry lips.

He inhaled sharply and put a hand out to touch her cheek.

"You are exquisite," he whispered, before stepping back.

He took his camera from the stand. "Take it off," he said gruffly.

As if in a trance, she complied. He stared transfixed. Someone shouted in the distance, and he lifted his camera. He started clicking away, and her body moved without any direction from him.

Somewhere, a voice was telling her she was supposed to

lie down so that she was covered in sand but the voice was very far away. Besides, she wasn't interested in listening to it anyway.

"Lie down," Darryn eventually said, his voice hoarse.

She sank down and stretched out on her tummy. And while the sun was setting, the waves crashing behind them, her body moved to the beat of her heart.

"Okay, that's it," he finally said and lifted his head. He picked up her top and, holding out his hand, he helped her up.

She pulled the top over her head.

"I want to see you tonight."

She didn't even think about refusing. "Yes."

"Room?"

"Twenty-two.

"Eight?"

"Yes."

His smile was devastating. Her knees nearly buckled.

"Good," he said and walked back to his camera stand.

The next minute, the rest of the crew surrounded them and everyone was talking and asking questions. Hannah floated back to the hotel, walking on air, her heart still hammering away.

She never dated photographers, never went out with them. It was a decision she made when she'd started. But there was no way she was saying no to Darryn Cavallo.

"Hi Hannah," a voice said behind her, and she put on a

fake smile before she looked over her shoulder.

"Hi," she tried to hold the smile but continued walking.

Stephen White gave her the willies. He was also a photographer, and she loathed working with him. He leered and was forever creeping up on her, brushing against her, and trying to get her to go out with him. She'd tried to be nice; she didn't want to antagonize anyone, but he was really beginning to be a pest.

Apparently, she wasn't the only model to feel this way about him. She'd made up her mind that if he tried to touch her inappropriately one more time, she was going to lodge a formal complaint.

"Why in such a hurry?" he said and grabbed her arm.

She sharply pulled back her arm. "I have a date tonight," she said and turned to leave.

He swore viciously. She ignored him and walked as quickly as she could toward the doors of the hotel.

"Do you honestly think you'll be the first model Darryn sleeps with?" he shouted after her, but she just kept on walking.

What a horrible, creepy man! She shuddered as she stepped into the elevator. She had no illusions about Darryn and knew this would be a one-night stand. But it also would be one night she'd never forget.

ON HIS WAY to Hannah's room, Darryn ran into Stephen

White. Stephen and he had gone to school together, and when the man had reached out to him a few years back, saying he was also into fashion photography and asked for help with contacts, he'd reluctantly agreed. They had never been friends but, because of their school ties, Darryn did what he could to help him find work.

But he didn't like the way the guy did things and stayed clear of him as much as possible. He nodded in Stephen's direction and hurried past him.

He was way too early, but he couldn't wait.

Everything he was going to say was clear in his head. This was a mistake, he couldn't stay, he'd forward her the photos, hoped to see her again sometime.

He should know better. He'd made the rookie mistake of falling for a model when he'd started in the business. And he'd been on his way to buy a ring when he discovered she'd been two-timing, or actually three-timing, him all along. This was a very temporary business, models came and went, and so did photographers. So he'd learned to appreciate the beauty around him, but to steer clear of entanglements. It was better for business, way better for his heart.

Besides, he'd been considering his brother Don's suggestions to join his hotel boutique business, and the more he thought about it, the more sense it made. His two other brothers, Dale and David, also seemed to be interested in joining Don. So to start a relationship or even just a fling at this point in his life simply didn't make sense.

But then, today, he'd walked down to the beach and seen a woman draped in tulle, twirling, her long blonde tresses flying about her face. And then she laughed, and his camera started clicking before he realized what he was doing.

Hannah Sutherland. He'd heard about her of course. Everyone in the fashion industry knew or had at least heard of this model who, within the span of merely a year, had media heads, photographers, agents, and event coordinators falling all over themselves to have her on covers, grace their tables, and make events worth attending.

He'd never quite understood the hype. Models were usually exceptionally beautiful, and he had become used to being among gorgeous, half-naked women most of his days without breaking out in a sweat. Hannah Sutherland would just be another model he had been asked to photograph.

But the moment he'd laid eyes on her, pieces of a messy puzzle that had been floating around him since forever finally fell into place, and something inside him went, *oh, there you are.* And from that moment, he hadn't been able to take his eyes off her.

Only after she'd left did he come out of his trance and realize to sleep with her would be repeating an old mistake. And he'd known if he were to be in the same room with her, alone, he would not be able to keep his hands to himself. He had to remember she was a model and probably had a string of lovers.

He could have sent her a message, probably should have.

But he owed her an explanation.

He reached her room and knocked on the door.

It opened, and every rational thought in his brain simply evaporated. Dressed in shorts and a halter top, her blonde hair falling messily around her, she simply took his breath away, scrambled his brain and his heart surrendered.

He stepped in, shut the door behind him, and then she was in his arms.

THERE WASN'T ANY time to catch her breath. She'd had a shower when she arrived in her room earlier, but she'd still been thinking about what to wear when there was a knock on her door.

She wasn't prepared to find Darryn already standing there—it was way too early. He was dressed in a white T-shirt and jeans, his eyes had turned to liquid chocolate, and her knees buckled beneath her. Before she could gather herself, his arms were around her, and he was kissing her like she had never been kissed before.

The smell of sunshine, summer, sandalwood, and spices surrounded her. Underneath her fingers, his heart tripped, her breath hitched in her throat as feeling took over from thinking, and her senses went into overload.

Her hands roamed over broad shoulders, reveled in the rippling of his muscles underneath her touch. She loved the hard contours of his magnificent body.

With a groan, he lifted his head. His eyes were smoldering as he gulped in air. "I'm sorry, I didn't mean to jump you."

She smiled, touching his face. "I'm not complaining."

The words popped out before she could think about what she was saying. She was never this brazen. She was the shy one, the quiet one. But apparently around Darryn Cavallo, she turned into a completely different person.

His eyes darkened. With unsteady fingers, he lifted her hair from her shoulders, fisted his hand around it.

"Are you sure?" he asked. "Because if I kiss you again, I won't stop. I don't usually sleep with models," he said and pressed her hair against his cheek, "but you…" His arms gathered her close.

"Well, then. What are you waiting for?" she whispered and boldly stepped between his legs. "And I… I've never slept with a photographer."

HE WAS A dead man. That was his last coherent thought before a red haze moved in front of his eyes, and the roaring in his ears made it impossible to think, to rationalize, to plan. Hannah fit perfectly against his body, as if she'd been made especially for him.

Without taking his mouth from hers, he moved backward until they both fell onto the bed. He kept her body above him and all that glorious blonde hair tumbled forward, cocooning them both inside a small world all their own.

He couldn't get enough of her. Unsteady, frantic hands got rid of clothing and he was finally able to touch her skin, discover the contours of her lithe body, delight in her feminine curves.

Shuddering, his hand found its way down to her heat. She was wet and ready for him, burning for him, and he was lost.

With her breath in his ear, her long legs wrapped around him, he pushed into her. Their eyes locked together. He tried to focus, he wanted to see every expression on her face, but her heat surrounded him and with a feral growl, he made her his. He buried his face in her neck, and while silently freaking out, swore he heard his heart shattering into a million pieces.

HANNAH'S EYES FLUTTERED open a little later and she realized she would never be the same again. Ever. She was a different person than she had been last night. Darryn's lovemaking had changed the beat of her heart, the rhythm of the way she breathed, had changed her very soul.

She turned her head. Dark brown eyes were watching her.

He smiled.

Her heart tripped. "Good morning."

Hesitantly, he touched her cheek. "You're real. For a minute there, I was wondering whether I was dreaming." His voice was liquid chocolate, his hand not quite steady.

She'd thought the fire he'd lit inside of her last night had died, but sizzling embers burst into flame again and she pulled his head down. Immediately a whirlwind swept her up again and she was lost.

HOURS LATER WHEN she opened her eyes again, he was dressed in only jeans and was opening the hotel room door.

"Yes, that looks great. Thanks." The next minute he pulled a trolley into the room. "Breakfast." He looked at his watch. "Or a late lunch, rather. I don't know about you, but I need food."

Hannah sat up and looked around for something to put on.

He grinned and tossed her his T-shirt. "I don't mind you being naked, but if you want to eat, you should probably put something on."

"Oh, I want to eat," she said and pulled the T-shirt over her head. It was way too big for her, but at least she was covered. It was difficult to act normal with his hot, brown eyes following her every move. She got out of the bed and moved toward the trolley.

"I wasn't sure whether you're a coffee or tea person, so I ordered both," he said.

"Coffee, please, when I wake up, tea the rest of the day,"

she said and poured herself a cup. "You?" She picked up the other cup.

"Coffee. Always. Can't stand tea."

"Coffee it is." She handed him his coffee and curled up in one of the chairs, her legs tucked away underneath her. "Favorite food?"

BY THE TIME the tray was empty, they'd discovered they both loved Italian food, listened to rock music, preferred a Shiraz when they drank wine, couldn't stand large crowds, and preferred to stay home rather than go out. She would watch the odd whodunit movie, but preferred sappy love stories; he, of course, preferred thrillers, war movies, and spy stories.

But it was getting more difficult by the minute to focus on her questions. She'd moved in the chair and now the T-shirt had ridden up her thigh. His eyes had zoomed in on her exposed satiny skin and her voice was coming from further and further away.

"Tell me about your family?" she asked.

He got up and went over to where she was sitting.

"You really want to talk about family?"

Her eyes darkened with desire. She lifted her arms. "Not really."

MUCH LATER, DARRYN lay staring at the ceiling. Next to him, Hannah was still sleeping. He turned his head. She was lying on her tummy, the whole of her naked smooth back exposed to him.

For three days, he'd hardly left her side.

They'd finished the shoot yesterday, and since then they'd hardly left her room. He couldn't get enough of her. Last night, he'd forced himself to take her out to dinner, but he couldn't keep his hands to himself, and they'd left before their food arrived.

He'd been with her for three days and three nights, damn it! Surely he should have had his fill by now? This had never happened to him before.

Usually, he was very happy to say goodbye to a woman after one night, never mind how mind-blowing the sex had been. But this time everything was different.

She'd filled every aching hole he'd ever had, stilled every craving, and had made every single boyhood fantasy came true. Every time she'd moved, he put out a hand to make sure she was real, and once he'd touched her, he had to have her again. And again.

She was nothing like anyone he'd known before. He didn't trust easily, but it was so easy to be with Hannah, to talk about himself, to share his thoughts and dreams.

And what they had together was so much more than mere sex—his mind, his soul, his very being became part of her.

He tried to take a breath, but it was difficult. Damn, he was freaking out. These feelings he was experiencing—they were too much, too intense, too bloody overpowering. What did he do with all of this?

He had to get out of here, away from her.

Thinking straight had been impossible over the last few days, and he needed to think. Silently, he got up and looked for his pants. Sneaking out after spending three days with a woman, having made love to her more times than he could count, was not something he thought he'd ever do.

But his mind and body were in overload and he needed to breathe. Somehow, he had to try and make sense of what he was feeling before he could speak to her again. Was this real, or was he simply imagining the strong connection they had?

Connection? Surely he couldn't have fallen in love with her within the span of three days? That didn't happen, right? After pulling on his pants, he grabbed his shirt while stepping into his shoes. Before he opened the door, he looked back at her again and very nearly walked back.

He quickly opened the door and stepped out, closing it behind him.

"A nice piece of ass, don't you agree?" he heard Stephen White's voice near him.

"What did you say?"

"Did you find the butterfly?" Stephen snickered and sauntered away.

Stunned, Darryn looked after him while rubbing his chest. A sharp object pierced right through his heart. He couldn't breathe.

Disappointment rose like bile and filled his belly. He grimaced. Damn, he'd gone and done it again—fell for a model. Would he never learn?

He'd found the butterfly all right, delighted in the tiny colorful mark on her butt. He thought he was the first to see it. But apparently not.

Coming to a quick decision, he walked briskly in the direction of his room while he took out his phone and punched in Don's telephone number. It was time to move on.

Dazed, Hannah stared at the door. Surely Darryn wouldn't believe the idiot? She pressed her ear to the door again, waiting for Darryn to say something, but the only sound was footsteps walking away.

How would Stephen know about her tattoo?

Of course. She and the other models had been talking about their secret tattoos just the other day and Stephen had to have been listening around the corner like he usually did.

She flung open the door, ready to run after Darryn, but the next minute Stephen pushed her back into the room.

"You piece of trash," he hissed. "You think I'm not good enough for you, but you spend time—"

Hannah didn't wait for him to finish. She aimed a kick at his groin, and while he was doubling up and cursing, she shoved him out of her room, locking the door behind her.

Her hands still shaking, she took out her phone. This had to stop today. Stephen White should have been fired long ago.

While the phone rang, she swallowed back the sob that was threatening to break loose. Her heart was breaking. The man she'd spent the last few days with, the man she'd lost her heart to within the span of seventy two hours, couldn't leave the room quickly enough this morning.

After the wonderful time they'd had over the past three days, Darryn had simply gotten up and walked out. The pain just below her heart was unexpected and so fierce she nearly doubled up.

Disillusioned and tired, she sank down on the bed, waiting for her agent to answer the phone.

She shouldn't be surprised about Darryn's behavior, though. Despite their romance-writing mother's best efforts to tell them otherwise, she and her two sisters knew how fickle men were. Their father hadn't even stayed around, but had left them when they were still in primary school.

At least now she had fresh information for her sister Caitlin's blog. She'd always felt kind of bad about the way Caitlin posted about all the terrible dates they'd been on, but her experience with Darryn Cavallo was probably one of the worst 'dates' she'd ever had with a man. He stayed with her for three days, left, and then believed the first lie he heard about her. If he hadn't believed the guy, he would have turned back and asked her about it, wouldn't he?

AS SHE STEPPED out of the elevator, Stephen was on his way to the big front doors of the hotel, suitcase in hand. She lifted her head and turned to walk to the dining room, but he grabbed her arm.

"You think you're in charge? You think you can get rid of me with one phone call to your agent? Well, I've got news for you. You might have gotten rid of me, but I am going to make your life a living nightmare, you hear me?" he hissed.

"I—"

Another stopped close by, and several of the other models entered the foyer.

Swearing, Stephen dropped her arm, and with a last furious scowl, walked out of the hotel.

Rattled and upset, Hannah turned and followed the other models into the dining room. As she entered the big room, her heart stopped for a moment. Darryn was on his way out.

He frowned when he saw her, and she waited for him to walk past her, but instead he stopped right in front of her. His demeanor was so different from that of the man with whom she'd spent the last few days, she couldn't get a word out.

He obviously didn't have the same problem. "Seriously?

Getting Stephen fired because he told me you sleep around? You lied to me!"

Stunned, she inhaled sharply. "I can't believe you listened to his lies. Not after the time we spent together. I don't sleep around, and as for getting Stephen fired—"

But Darryn put his fingers on her lips and grimaced. "No more lies, please. I've had a good time, let's leave it at that." He shook his head. "You took me by surprise. I've never…" He frowned and started to turn away.

Hannah grabbed his hand. "Never what?" she asked breathlessly, a faint glimmer of hope looming. Maybe…

He shook off her hand. "Forget it. You are obviously not who I thought you were." With those words, he turned around and walked away.

"Neither were you," she got out. He turned back to her and she shrugged. "You left me this morning even before you listened to Stephen's nonsense. You didn't have to sneak out, you could have told me you'd had enough."

"I didn't—" he began to say, but bit off the words. The next minute he was gone.

SHE HEARD LATER that morning that Darryn had quit his job to join his brothers in a business venture. He'd left the hotel, the island, her life.

She was numb. Three days ago she'd met this man. She'd given him her body, her soul, and, she realized now, her heart. But he'd walked out this morning without a word of explanation. And then he was quick to believe what Stephen White told him about her.

She wanted to crawl into the nearest hole and cry herself to sleep, but she was flying back to South Africa today. She squared her shoulders, lifted her chin, and discovered throughout the course of the day that one could actually function quite well with a broken heart.

The one bright spot in her day was that Stephen White was also gone. She heard the other models whispering about it and a few thanked her for getting rid of him. She was not the only one he'd been pestering.

Chapter Two

The present

"OKAY, I'M NEARLY done. I'll send the photos in about half an hour," Darryn said to his brother Don over the phone before he ended the call.

He was working on photos for the new brochures and website for their new hotel close to the Kruger National Park. He'd spent weeks in and around the park to get photographs of the so-called big five—the African lion, the African elephant, the Cape buffalo, the African leopard, and the white and black rhinoceros.

Hunters had coined the phrase "big five" because these animals were so difficult to hunt, and he quickly realized that for his kind of shooting, they also presented a challenge.

They were beautiful creatures, and he could never shoot them with a gun, but with a camera, he could show the world their habitat, portray exactly how magnificent they were. Rhinoceros poaching was a huge problem, and he and his brothers were doing their little bit to try to prevent poachers from getting to these animals, at least, on the land surrounding their hotel.

He turned back to his laptop, and his fingers accidentally touched his keypad. And the next minute a beautiful woman twirling in a tulle skirt filled his screen. Swearing, he stared at her laughing face.

Damn it, he'd inadvertently opened the file with the photos he'd taken of Hannah Sutherland two years ago.

These particular photographs hadn't been part of the brief that day, so he hadn't needed to send them on to the client or to Hannah. He also hadn't needed to keep them on his laptop. He even had a blown-up print of this particular photo. One that he hid behind a cupboard in his bedroom. He should have gotten rid of these photos and of the print a long ago, except…

Staring into her beautiful blue eyes, he could vividly remember every single second he'd spent with her. He still had explicit dreams of their lovemaking, of her long limbs entwined around him, his whole being immersed in her scent.

When he'd walked out of Hannah's life and away from his job as a fashion photographer, he figured he'd never see her again in the flesh. Her face would be everywhere—she was the new darling of the catwalks, of magazines, after all. Her picture graced covers, posters, even lit up some buildings.

He never meant to buy all the magazines with her on the cover and was amazed by the stack in his bedroom.

And then, in a cruel twist of fate, two of her sisters and

one of their best friends were now married to his three brothers! It was so bizarre. He had still been trying to come to grips with the fact that his big brother Don had fallen for Caitlin, Hannah's older sister, when Dale started acting all weird and out of sorts, until he put his ring on Zoe, the other sister. And if that hadn't been enough, David had found his soul mate in Dana, Caitlin's best friend.

Uncomfortable, Darryn shifted on his chair. After all this time, after everything he knew about her, Hannah still managed to get him all hot and bothered. He still couldn't believe she'd slept with Stephen White, of all people. There had been times over the past two years when he'd wondered if the guy had told him that out of spite, but then he remembered the damn tattoo. There was no way anyone could know about the tiny butterfly without having seen it.

Ever since he'd joined Don and his brothers at the firm, he'd made a conscious effort to date as many women as possible in the hope he'd find at least one who might pique his interest. But to no avail. None of them had been able to even vaguely interest him, let alone make him forget Hannah.

And ever since Don and Caitlin came together, family meetings tended to include the Sutherlands as well, and that meant Hannah was suddenly part of his life.

He still wanted her. Despite knowing she hadn't been honest when she'd said she never slept with photographers. The fact that she'd jumped into bed with Stephen bloody

White wasn't something he could get his head around. The guy was plain creepy.

He had tried to warn Don and Dale not to trust the Sutherland sisters. Of course, nobody listened to him, and he had grudgingly come to realize just how wrong he had been about his new sisters-in-law—they were in a league of their own. And this, of course, led him to wonder whether he'd been correct in his assessment of Hannah.

But how else would the guy know about the tattoo?

He was desperately trying to hang onto his anger and hurt; he kept reminding himself she was not who he'd initially thought, but his body completely ignored all his rational arguments.

Whenever he got close to her, his cave instincts kicked in, and he wanted to protect, to possess, to claim, to kiss. Damn it to hell, what was it with this woman?

The more he saw of Hannah, the more he realized he liked her. She was quiet, listened rather than talked, and really cared about her family, about his family. The only time her smile slipped was when her gaze landed on him.

Watching his brothers was not helping his frustration. They were all blissfully happy.

Sickeningly so. They all obviously adored their wives. And he had started to look forward to the many family gatherings. He liked his new sisters-in-law and had become a huge fan of Brenda, the mother of the three sisters.

Could he have been wrong? Maybe he should do what he

should have done two years ago and ask Hannah about the whole thing.

Frowning, he closed the file. That was, if he saw her again. She hadn't been around over the last few months. She hadn't even gone to David's wedding to Dana. And damn it to hell, he missed her!

And the strange accidents that kept happening around her had him on edge. Every single time he heard that Hannah had been in or near an accident, his heart seemed to stop. It scared the living daylights out of him that something might happen to her.

At first he'd thought she was just careless, but he was worried enough to ask security to make sure she didn't leave the hotel unattended while she was on the island of Mahé in the Seychelles. And of course, she and Zoe managed to ditch them and slip away. That was the night Zoe had nearly been trampled by a crowd. And he then realized there was more to it than what Hannah wanted to reveal.

He'd asked her sisters; they were as worried as he was, but she hadn't told them anything he didn't know about.

Shrugging, he opened the file he was supposed to be working on. She was probably being wined and dined by some billionaire.

But half an hour later, he was still staring at the computer screen, not having done a thing.

WITH TREMBLING FINGERS, Hannah locked the door of her Paris apartment behind her when she got in and, frantically pulling the scarf from around her neck, leaned against the front door for a moment. The despair she kept pushing away soared to the surface and, for the first time in two years, the tears she'd been battling to keep down spilled over.

It was never going to stop. When Stephen White had threatened he to make her life a living nightmare two years ago, he hadn't been joking.

What he'd failed to mention at the time was that she would never feel safe again. And, as she had discovered to her horror, neither would people close to her or even colleagues who happened to have a similar build to hers.

Poor, poor Sophie. How was she to know the reason she'd been shoved in front of a car and nearly run over was because she had been mistaken for Hannah?

Hannah and three other models had just finished a shoot and were crossing the road. They were all dressed in jeans, white T-shirts, and bright yellow scarves. Sophie, who had a very similar build to Hannah, had been walking slightly in front of the rest of them.

Hannah had bent down to adjust her shoe when she heard Sophie's scream and the sound of a car skidding to a stop. She looked up just in time to see Sophie's yellow scarf falling, falling, falling.

And she immediately knew what had happened. Stephen had to be around and had mistaken Sophie for her. That was why Sophie had been shoved in front of the car. If the driver hadn't swerved…

Hannah tried to control herself, but a sob escaped, and she clamped a hand over her mouth. Inhaling through her nose, she concentrated on her breathing, desperately trying to remember something, anything good.

She missed her sisters, missed her mother, missed her new brothers-in-law, and she missed South Africa. But while Stephen was out to hurt her in any way possible, she'd been staying as far away from them as possible.

She hadn't even tried to attend Dana's wedding to David Cavallo. Although Dana was her sister's Caitlin's best friend, she had become like a sister to all of them. Stephen would have known about it, and he would have been waiting at the airport as he'd been doing for the past two years.

She still wasn't sure how he managed to always know where she would be, but she could assume he still had contact with some of the models. It could also be that he still had contact with Darryn Cavallo.

Darryn. Another sob threatened to escape, and she gulped in deep breaths. After all this time, she was still shocked that Darryn had chosen to believe what Stephen had to say about her, even after they had spent the most wonderful, earth-shattering days and nights of passion together.

It had to be the irony of all ironies that two of her sisters were now married to two of his brothers. Suddenly, he was part of her life again.

And even though he obviously still believed Stephen's

lies about her, he kept kissing her. Like the time in the airport on Mahé and while he was dancing with her during her sisters' weddings. How was she supposed to understand such a man?

Hannah slowly got up and, still shivering, walked to her room. Sleep was nearly impossible nowadays and tonight she would not be able to close her eyes. All she could see was the yellow scarf falling, falling, falling.

She left her phone on the bedside table, pulled off her jeans, and crept under the duvet.

After she realized Stephen was, in fact, stalking her, she'd changed her phone number frequently, but he always had his way of finding out what it was, so she'd stopped changing it, and now she simply never answered calls from an unknown number.

Her eyes closed. In slow motion, the afternoon scene replayed itself in her mind's eye. It had been such a lovely day and a fun-filled shoot. For a few minutes she'd actually forgotten about Stephen and his threats.

It was time to get security or something. She kept hoping Stephen would find someone else to bother, but she had now finally realized he wasn't going to stop of his own accord.

Another sob escaped, and she sat up just as her phone started ringing. It was her sister Caitlin. She probably shouldn't answer, because Caitlin would immediately know something was wrong. But if she didn't pick up, her sister would worry. Hannah inhaled deeply, put a smile on her face, and answered the phone.

Chapter Three

DARRYN WASN'T SURE why he was there. But somehow, being close to one of Hannah's sisters always seemed to calm him down. He was feeling restless, kind of anxious, and he wasn't sure why. He'd been working nonstop to get photos ready for the launch of their new hotel, and everything was running smoothly.

He hadn't been sleeping well; he couldn't stop thinking about Hannah. Nothing new—he was always thinking about her. But ever since the thought of asking her about Stephen White had popped up in his head, he kept coming back to the idea.

Over the last few days, his restlessness had increased, and with it, a feeling of dread kept him on edge. It was taking all his self-control not to jump on their company plane and go find Hannah. He'd hoped, maybe here, close to her sister, he'd be more settled. And maybe he'd hear something about Hannah's whereabouts without having to ask.

"You look like hell," said Don as they hugged.

Darryn shrugged and ignored the statement. "What are you doing all alone on a Saturday night?" Don asked as they entered the big living room.

A television was on and Darryn glanced at the flashing pictures. It was on a fashion channel, he would know; he watched it often enough. In the corner of the room, a huge square box was filled to the rim with toys.

"Just stopping by," he said easily. "Donato asleep already?"

The stupid grin Don usually got when anyone talked about his son appeared immediately. "Yes, the little guy attended his first party today and fell asleep on the way home."

"You'll have to work on his stamina. In your heyday, you could party all night long." Grinning, Darryn motioned toward the television. "And look what you're now doing on a Saturday night."

"Caitlin was watching the Paris Fashion Show. Hannah was one of the models. And then, of course, she had to talk to her on the phone right away." He frowned. "We haven't heard from Hannah in a while. Caitlin is still surprised she didn't even attend Dana and David's wedding and she's worried about her, has been for some time now."

Darryn rubbed his chest where the feeling of dread was more acute now.

"Don!" Caitlin's anxious voice sounded down the corridor, and the next minute she was standing in the door, her eyes brimming with tears. She glanced in Darryn's direction and nodded, but she walked into Don's open arms.

"What's wrong?" asked Don.

"It's Hannah. Something is very, very wrong, but she—" She suddenly stopped speaking, stepped out of Don's arms while grabbing the television remote. The voice that had been faint in the background now filled the entire room.

"It has been confirmed that it was Sophie Thomas who was pushed in front of a car, not Hannah Sutherland, as previously reported."

Darryn's heart simply stopped when he heard Hannah's name and "pushed in front of a car" in one sentence. His heart was beating so loudly, it blocked out the rest of the guy's words.

Caitlin turned around to Don, her face paling.

Darryn took a deep breath and tried to concentrate on what Caitlin was saying. He had to know what was going on.

"So that's what happened," she whispered. "I could tell something was wrong, but she kept saying she's fine. That's it! I'm flying to Hannah tonight…"

Don hugged her close, caressing her shoulders. "Of course, sweetheart, whatever you want, but let's talk about this," he said calmly and rationally. "We know Hannah is fine. She wasn't the person who was pushed. You spoke to her, you heard her voice, she's okay. What did she say to have you in tears?"

Flabbergasted, Darryn stared at Don. His mouth was so dry, he struggled to get words out. "She's really fine?" he finally managed.

Don nodded. "It was another model; she's fine too, by the way." He turned Caitlin back to face him. "Sweetheart, what—"

"She didn't really say anything, but I could hear she's been crying. And I'm sorry, but I can't believe all these things happening around Hannah are accidents!" Caitlin hiccupped and pushed away from Don. "I mean, after the first hit-and-run accident she had on Mahé, we all thought it was random, but then Zoe was pushed while she and Hannah were wearing similar-colored clothes, and now this. And there has to be a reason why Hannah didn't attend Dana and David's wedding."

Darryn heard Caitlin's voice as if from a distance. She was saying what had been bothering him for months now.

"But Hannah keeps saying nothing is wrong," Don said and led his wife to the couch.

"We've all been so busy falling in love and getting married, I think we all knew something was wrong, but we didn't push Hannah. I know something happened to her two years ago—she was devastated and hid away at my mom's for weeks. She didn't want to talk about it, though, and I always hoped she'd talk when she was ready." She stared at Don. "You know, now that I think about it, it was after those weeks she stayed with Mom that all these 'accidents' started to happen."

"So what? You think it has to do with whatever upset her in the first place?" asked Don.

Caitlin nodded. "It has to be. I mean Hannah is the quiet one, the happy one. But ever since that time, she has changed." She sighed and leaned against Don. Her gaze landed on Darryn and she pointed at him.

"Whatever happened to her then had something to do with you. That much I do know. Maybe it's time you tell us."

Darryn walked to a chair next to the couch and sat down. She was right; it was time to tell Caitlin what had happened between him and Hannah.

TEN MINUTES LATER Caitlin sat staring at him, her mouth open in shock.

"And you believed that...that idiot of a man?" she whispered. "No wonder she can't stand the sight of you! You said you spent three days and nights with her. You should have known by that time what kind of person my sister is. How could you believe someone else's lies about her?"

Darryn jumped up. "I..." He rubbed the back of his neck.

Don came to his rescue. "He had a nasty experience with another model, one who did sleep around."

"And I know Stephen White. He and I went to school together. I never much liked him, but I helped him get a few jobs...he was very grateful. I had no reason not to believe what he told me."

"Well, for your information, Hannah is incapable of two-timing anyone. She doesn't have a devious bone in her body! And you should know that!" Caitlin scolded. "She will kill me if I tell you this, but she funds a charity for war orphans! That's the kind of person she is!"

Stunned, Darryn stared at her. He hadn't known that about Hannah. Come to think of it, he didn't know anything about her life apart from the fact she was a model.

Caitlin stood up as well, glaring at him. She wiped her wet cheeks, her eyes shooting darts in his direction. "You could easily have found out anything about Hannah's life—every detail is on the Internet. But you jumped to conclusions and probably never even bothered to ask her side of the story."

"He knew about her tattoo!" Darryn shouted.

Caitlin eyes became slits. It was obvious she knew what he was talking about. "And of course the only way he could know about it was if he saw it?" she said, not even trying to hide the sarcasm in her voice.

"Well, yes! I thought…what we had was special. I fell for her. Big time!"

Don snickered. "I knew it!" he said slapping his knee.

Caitlin stared at Darryn for long minutes, and then the ghost of a smile lifted the corners of her mouth. "So that's what happened. Typical. You freaked out. When you realized how you felt about her, you freaked out and jumped at the chance to believe the drivel this Stephen told you, that way you didn't have to deal with your feelings. You could just walk away feeling all righteous and indignant—typical Cavallo move, by the way. Am I right?" she asked crossing her arms.

"Hey—I saw the light eventually," Don complained with a smile. "And so did David and Dale. It's just this poor sod here who doesn't know what hit him."

Darryn started pacing. "But the tattoo—" he began again.

Caitlin grabbed his arm, bringing him to a standstill. "I don't know how he knew about it, but I can assure you, he didn't see it." She dropped her hand and faced Don again. "I don't have time to try to convince your brother of something he should have known to be untrue. I have to get to Hannah. I should have listened to my gut a long time ago. And what it's been telling me is that something is very, very wrong."

"I'll go," Darryn said. "I can go immediately. Whatever I need to do, I can do from anywhere. You are a family—it's going to take time to get everyone ready, but I can leave right now. Come when you're ready. I have a Euro Visa, and I can pack quickly."

"She doesn't want to see you," Caitlin said.

"Well, that's too damn bad, because I'm going to see her. I want to know...I *need* to know she's safe," he ended fiercely.

Caitlin walked up to him, one finger in the air. "If you do or say anything to upset her, I'll put both our mothers onto you," she threatened.

"I can't promise you I won't upset her," he said, "but I can promise you I'll do my best to get to the bottom of this."

But Caitlin had turned back and was facing the television again. Don had turned up the volume.

"…Not Hannah Sutherland, but Sophie Thomas, who has a similar build…"

"Looks like they've been repeating the news," Don said.

"They didn't mention before that this woman has a similar build to Hannah," Darryn said frowning.

Caitlin stared at the screen. "So Hannah could have been the target?" she whispered the words they were all thinking.

It was quiet in the room for a few seconds.

Then he and Don turned to one another. "Get security for her," Darryn barked while he took out his phone.

Don pushed him in the direction of the front door. "I'll inform David and Dale you have the plane," he said, his cell phone also in his hand. "Send it back as soon as possible. Caitlin and I will follow when we're ready."

Caitlin grabbed Darryn's hand. "You make sure she's safe, okay?" she said in a wobbly voice.

Darryn bent down and gave her a hug. "That I can promise," he said before a voice answered on the other side of the line.

"I need the plane. Immediately," he said, and with a last wave, sprinted toward his car.

Chapter Four

HANNAH OPENED HER eyes, hanging on to that perfect moment between sleep and reality where everything was entirely fine, where no worry or anxiousness intruded, where she could simply be.

But then she blinked, reality came crashing down, and she was fully awake. Immediately, the feeling of dread, of fear, had her tummy tied in knots.

A loud noise made her sit upright. That was what had woken her. Someone was hammering against her front door. She grabbed her gown and glanced at her watch. It was nearly eleven o'clock. Normally, she wouldn't still be in bed, but she'd only fallen asleep in the early morning hours.

She really hoped it wasn't the police. They'd phoned yesterday, asking her if she wanted to file a complaint; apparently the story of Sophie's near-accident had hit the news. She told them she'd see them sometime today, hoping to delay having to talk about the incident again.

Fortunately, she only had an appointment after lunch with a photographer who did a cover shoot with her last week. She wasn't quite sure why he wanted to meet again, but her agent asked nicely, and she wanted to keep the client happy.

The hammering continued. Irritated, she walked toward the front door. The block of apartments she lived in had security downstairs, so whoever was knocking had to be someone she'd cleared with them. It could also be someone from her agency. Why the idiot didn't stop hammering, though, she couldn't imagine.

She didn't even look through the peephole, just flung the door open, ready to give whoever was standing there hell. Her words disappeared, as did all the oxygen around her.

Standing on her doorstep, unshaven, drop-dead gorgeous, his eyes red-rimmed, was Darryn Cavallo.

Before she could get anything out, his strong arms folded around her, and he kicked the door shut behind him. He was trembling as he pulled her close to his body.

She tried to push him away even though her body ached for his heat. She was so cold. But this was Darryn Cavallo, the guy who'd broken her heart and stomped all over it.

He ignored her movements, though, gathered her closer, and pressed his face into her neck. "We heard what happened yesterday. Heard the woman had a similar build to you, realized it could have been you. I need to hold you for a few moments...please?"

His unique scent of sandalwood and spices surrounded her, and she nodded. Her arms found their way around him, and for a long moment they stood like that. She sighed and he pressed a kiss to her forehead. She didn't know why he was there, what he wanted, but she felt safe. For the first time in a long time.

"I need a shower, and then we have to talk," he said gruffly and dropped his arms.

Immediately, she shivered. She was so cold again.

"Hannah," Darryn said and tried to pull her into his arms again.

But she stepped away and crossed her arms. "There are two spare bedrooms on your left, each with a bathroom. Choose either one. I…" She looked down at herself, realizing for the first time that she was still in her pajamas.

"I…" she tried again and looked up into his face. A big mistake. "I also have to shower and get dressed," she whispered.

His eyes darkened as they swept over her and the tiny muscle in his cheek jumped.

His eyes were black when they reached hers again. "Then you better do it quickly before I forget about the rest of the world and undress you all the way."

His huskily whispered words inflamed her already heightened senses and she turned around and fled to her room.

DARRYN SWORE AS he walked toward the spare bedroom. Damn it to hell! He was like a bloody hormone-driven teenager around this woman. He was here to try and figure out what was going on in her life, who wanted to hurt her, and the only thing he could think of when she opened the door, looking all rumpled and sexy, was getting her in a bed and out of the few scraps of clothing she was wearing as soon as possible.

He closed the door behind him while he was still cussing. Sleep had been impossible last night. Normally, he didn't have a problem and could sleep in any position in any place, but he was so worried and anxious about Hannah, he couldn't close his eyes. So now he couldn't think straight, and being this close to Hannah wasn't helping.

The security guard had already been outside her door when he arrived. The guy had insisted on seeing Darryn's passport, and although he hated the time he wasted doing that, at least he knew the guard was doing his job.

He'd wait for Don and Caitlin to tell her about the security detail that would be following her every movement from now on. The Sutherland women were fiercely independent, and he could just imagine Hannah's reaction.

He opened the brand-new suitcase he'd bought on the airport when he landed in Paris earlier and grabbed some of the clothes he'd picked up in a hurry. Whatever else he might need, he'd get later in the day. To reach Hannah as soon as possible had been his goal; he didn't want to waste time going back to his house to pack clothes.

As he stepped into the bathroom, he heard it—the sound

of another shower right on the other side of this damn wall! Swearing a blue streak, he opened the taps. Cold water cascaded over his overheated body and another string of curses followed. This bloody woman was going to be the death of him yet.

AS SHE STEPPED out of her room, Darryn closed the door of the spare room behind him. He was scowling. When he saw her, the scowl deepened.

"Why are you glaring at me?" she asked and walked past him with her head held high. "Nobody asked you to come here; you can't be irritated with me in my own home."

The next minute he'd pinned her against the wall. Darryn leaned into her, close enough so that she could feel... Her eyes widened.

"Precisely." He growled. "That's what you do to me. You wet and naked on the other side of that damn wall? You should be glad scowling is all I'm doing," he said, before he turned around and walked away toward the kitchen.

On unsteady legs, Hannah followed him. The man still managed to jumpstart all of her senses with merely a whisper.

As she walked into the kitchen, she could hear the kettle had been switched on and Darryn was opening and closing cupboard doors.

"Sit down, I'll do it," she said and moved around the kitchen counter. It was necessary for her to keep her hands busy, otherwise she might just do something ridiculous like throw her arms around Darryn.

"Don and Caitlin are on their way. Rather than wait for the company plane I took to return, they decided to fly commercial and will let me know when they'll be arriving," Darryn said behind her.

Hannah swallowed a few times, trying to get rid of the huge lump in her throat. Caitlin had tried to talk to her on numerous occasions over the past two years, had asked what was wrong, but Hannah hadn't wanted to bother her sisters with what she thought was something that would go away. She probably should have spoken sooner, at least told her family what was going on.

"Hannah," Darryn said behind her, but she couldn't turn around, couldn't speak.

The spoons in her hand dropped and, startled, she jumped away. Her nerves were shot. The next minute, two arms folded around her from behind and held her tightly.

"I…" she began, but her throat clogged up.

Cussing, Darryn turned her around and picked her up. With long strides, he walked to the couch and sat down, cradling her in his arms. And everything she had been bottling up over the past two years simply erupted. She fell against him with a sob and burst out crying.

Darryn tucked her head under his chin and began to stroke her hair with one hand while the other held her tightly against his body. The tears wouldn't stop, and she gave up trying to hold herself together, pressing her face against Darryn's broad chest, and cried.

⭐

DARRYN HUGGED HER slender body against his, vowing to find out who was causing Hannah so much pain, if it was the last thing he did. Her every sob echoed through his body, her every shudder broke his heart.

Eventually she sat upright and grabbed a tissue from the side table.

"I'm sorry, I don't usually…" she began, but he put his fingers on her lips.

"Don't apologize for crying, please. But tell me what the hell is going on. I refuse to believe that all these accidents are random, that it's a coincidence you are always around when someone gets hurt. Please talk to me."

Hannah jumped up and started pacing.

"You won't believe me. I don't want to believe me. It's one of those things you read about in a book or see in a movie—it doesn't happen to you."

"Try me," he said and willed himself not to get up and pull her into his arms again. She looked so lost, so…so…frightened.

She paused for a few seconds and looked at him before she resumed her pacing. She glanced at her watch and stopped quickly.

"I…have an appointment. I have to go," she said.

"What appointment?" he asked.

She lifted her chin. "Not that it's any of your business…"

The next minute, he grabbed her shoulders and pulled her closer. "Not my business?" he snarled. "When I can't stop thinking about you, stop worrying about you? Stop wanting you?"

Before she could utter a word, he crushed her against him and caught her lips with his. She tried to pull away, but he wasn't letting her go yet.

She gasped for air; he heightened the kiss and plunged his tongue deep while teasing and tormenting hers.

Gasping, she pushed him away, shaking her head.

"We can't do this. You make me…I…"

Frustrated, he hauled her closer. It had been supposed to be a quick kiss, meant to punish her. But the minute he tasted her, he lost whatever control he had over his feelings.

She was all sexy angles and smooth skin, all woman and heat, and he was slowly losing his mind. With a gasp, he lifted his head and cupped her face with unsteady hands.

"You will be the death of me yet." He growled, brushing back her hair. He had to clear his throat, speaking was difficult. "Now that we've established you are, in fact, my business," he said while taking her long hair into his fist, "tell me about this appointment."

HANNAH SWALLOWED AND, crossing her arms, moved away. He dropped his hands.

"I…it's a…" She took a deep breath, tried to focus on her words.

Kissing Darryn Cavallo wasn't something she should be doing, let alone be enjoying!

"I did a shoot for a magazine cover last week. The photographer wants to see me again."

He cocked his head and frowned. "Does that happen often?"

Chewing her lip, she slowly shook her head. "No, not really. But I've never worked with this guy before and maybe that's what he normally does. I don't know. I show up where I'm told to be."

He nodded, his mind working overtime.

Something didn't sound right, but the last thing he wanted to do was to upset Hannah further. Her phone rang, and she walked away while answering it.

He moved closer to the window that looked out over Paris. The city of love. Inside him, something shifted.

A little to his right was the Eiffel Tower and, far below, groups of tourists flocked in that direction. It was the beginning of spring, still cold outside, but the promise of warmer weather was in the air.

He stood staring through the window. Behind him, Hannah was talking softly. He was listening to her voice, not to what she was saying.

And then, whatever had shifted inside him seconds ago settled comfortably, and he knew. This was where he wanted to be. Close to her. Always. He loved her. He'd lost his heart to her on a sunny beach on Mahé two years ago, and that had never changed and it never would.

He turned around and looked at her. Really looked at her. He grinned. He loved watching her. Even when he'd been wracked with jealousy, when he'd been angry with her, his eyes would search a room full of people—for her. Even when he knew she wasn't there, he'd look for her.

She combed her fingers through her long blonde tresses and he struggled to get oxygen into his lungs. Her unique scent of roses with a hint of citrus wafted his way and he stopped worrying about breathing—he didn't need anything else, he could merely inhale her.

She was gorgeous; he'd always known that. Two years ago, he'd learned everything about her body in three days, but he'd walked away before he could get to know her mind, her heart, her soul.

And now that he knew how easily she loved, how deeply she cared, he realized Caitlin had been right—he should have acknowledged all of this two years ago.

Of course, he'd known what kind of person she was after spending time with her, but the intense feelings he'd experienced had been so powerful, so overwhelming, he'd opted to grab onto the first excuse to walk away and not deal with his emotions.

Stephen White had provided that excuse. But if the man had been lying—which at this point, Darryn had to admit, seemed be the case—the question was why? And damn it to hell, how had he known about the tattoo?

She ended her call and stood quietly, looking lost and vulnerable.

With two strides, he had her in his arms. "It's high bloody time for you to tell me exactly what the hell is going on."

She nodded, and a sob escaped against his neck at the same time someone knocked on her front door.

"Hannah, it's Caitlin!"

Hannah lifted her head with a wobbly smile, wiped her eyes, and ran toward the front door. She flung it open, and her sister caught her in a hug.

Chapter Five

"START RIGHT AT the beginning," Caitlin demanded. "Why do you think this photographer—what's his name? Stephen White?—is behind everything that has been happening to you?"

Don had made coffee and they were all sitting in the loving room.

Hannah glanced at Darryn. "I got him fired because... well, because he was pestering me, behaving inappropriately, and...the point is, he threatened to make my life hell and that's what he's been doing."

"So the hit and run accident in Mahé was him?" Caitlin asked incredulously.

"Well, initially I thought it was just an accident. But then he sent me a text message saying he was sorry to hear about the accident and that I should be more careful—anything could happen, any time."

Darryn jumped up. "Why didn't you tell anyone about it?"

"I thought he was just a nuisance, but then..."

"Zoe was pushed into a crowd while you and she were

having a good time in Mahé. I—" began Caitlin.

"Which, by the way, wouldn't have happened if you'd stayed in the hotel like I asked," Darryn interrupted. He knew he should keep quiet, but he couldn't believe what he was hearing.

Hannah gave him a cool look. "You didn't ask. You ordered two security guards to prevent us from leaving the hotel."

Don slapped him on the back, chuckling. "Oh, man, you still have a lot to learn."

Darryn shrugged off his brother's hand. Hell, he was only trying to protect her.

"So what exactly happened the night Zoe got hurt?" Caitlin asked.

"I saw him out of the corner of my eye while Zoe and I were having a drink. I was frantically trying to get us to safety, but Zoe and I got separated. He struck out at her, thinking it was me. We were wearing similar clothing. That was when I knew he was the one responsible for the hit and run, and I realized Zoe and I weren't safe."

Hannah glanced over at him, her eyes filled with remorse. "And you were right. Tt was my fault Zoe was hurt and I still feel terrible about it."

Caitlin glared at him while she spoke to Hannah. "It certainly wasn't your fault. Don't even think that. This guy is obviously unstable. Nothing that happened is of your doing, please remember that."

Darryn rubbed his face. Yeah, he knew that now, but at the time he was so upset that Hannah was hurt, he'd lashed out at her. Instead of being nice, he scolded.

He wanted to punch something. If he could get his hands on Stephen White. He had never liked the guy, but he never thought White would stoop this low.

"Well, I have to agree with you," Don said. "It has to be him."

Hannah crossed her arms. "I should have taken his threats seriously, but I honestly didn't think he was capable of being this vindictive. He never admits to anything in his text messages, of course, but he always knows exactly what has happened, and somehow he knows my every move!" Hannah exclaimed, and Caitlin took her hand.

Darryn looked at his brother and sister-in-law. "She hasn't told you everything, though. She left out that she got him fired right after the three days we spent together."

Hannah's mouth dropped open. "You told them about us?"

"Yes, he did, and now I understand so much better why you were so upset two year ago!" Caitlin exclaimed. "And don't worry," she said, giving Darryn a look. "I've told him exactly what an idiot he was to believe the drivel this White guy said about you."

"What do you know about White, apart from the fact that you and he went to the same school? You were obviously very quick to believe everything he said."

Darryn rubbed his face. "I never even liked the guy. And you're right, I shouldn't have been so quick to believe him. He was always into computers, and everyone assumed that's what he would go into. Then one day he phoned me out of the blue, said he was also a fashion photographer, and could I help him with contacts. So I did."

He thought of something and looked at Hannah. "You and I spent three days together, and then you got White fired. Why then?"

Hannah lifted an eyebrow. "Oh, now you want to listen to what I have to say?"

Darryn sighed. "I'm sorry, okay? I shouldn't have believed the guy, but he—"

"Told you about my tattoo and you believed him," Hannah said.

"I...yes. I...how did he know about it?" He held his breath.

"Darryn!" Caitlin scolded.

Hannah looked at him, ignoring her sister. "If you listened to me two years ago, I could have told you the truth then, but you—"

"I know, okay? I know," he said.

Hannah glared at him, but continued talking. "Some of the other models and I were joking about our secret tattoos at some point during our stay on Mahé. Stephen was forever listening around corners or peeping through holes, and that was probably how he'd heard about it. I can promise you, I'd rather slit my own throat than let that idiot touch me." She shuddered. "I've never met such a creepy man in my life!"

"So why did you wait until that day to lay a complaint against him?" Darryn asked. He frowned. "And how did you know he told me about your tattoo? Did he tell you?"

"Because…" Hannah began, but she swallowed and looked down at her clasped hands. "I heard you talking to him outside my door. I heard what he told you, I heard you walking away. I stupidly thought that if I ran after you, I could convince you he was lying, that he never saw my tattoo. But when I opened the door, he…he was right there. He pushed me back into the room…"

Furious, Darryn jumped up, his hands in fists. "What?"

"I didn't think, I just reacted. I kicked him in the groin, shoved him out of my room, and phoned my agent." She looked up. "And that's what got him fired. Not the fact that he told you I sleep around. Which, by the way, isn't true."

Darryn looked her straight in the eye. "I knew that. I…I was just so freaked out by the—"

"It happened a long time ago. Forget about it." Hannah waved his words away before he could finish.

"We are going to get to the bottom of this. At least you have security now," Caitlin said fervently and hugged Hannah close.

Hannah pushed her away. "What security?"

Caitlin looked in Darryn's direction and lifted an eyebrow. "You didn't tell her?"

Darryn cleared his throat and studied his fingers. "Thought it would be best coming from you."

"Yeah, right," Caitlin said with a knowing look.

She took Hannah's hands in hers. "You are in danger. You know that, we know that. Don and Darryn organized security outside your door. Someone will always be around and will escort you wherever you need to go."

Hannah shook her head, clearly upset. "I've thought about security too, but I don't want someone following me around! That's no way to live."

Don took a seat next to his wife. "We know. But what's the alternative? This guy isn't going to stop any time soon, until he's in custody. Please accept it?"

"Please?" Caitlin said. "I didn't tell Mom we were going to visit you, but she's going to find out within the next few hours that I'm here with you…"

Caitlin's phone rang and, grinning, she stood up. "And there she is," she said and walked away to answer.

TEARS WELLED UP again and Hannah angrily wiped them away. Crying wasn't going to stop Stephen White, wasn't going to change what was going on in his twisted mind.

Life had to go on. She looked at her watch. "I have to leave for my appointment, otherwise I'm going to be so late." She stood up and looked around, trying to think in spite of the nagging fear that something was about to happen. "My bag…" She remembered. "I need to get my bag."

"You are not going alone," Darryn said.

Hannah sighed in frustration. "This is work—I don't want a damn security guard following me around."

"Then I'm going with you," Darryn said and got up as well.

"Going where?" Caitlin asked as she walked back into the room.

"I have an appointment—it's about work."

"She's not going alone, I—"

"We'll all go," Caitlin said and picked up her bag. Don also got up.

"That's not—" Hannah began, but Caitlin lifted her chin stubbornly.

"We're here, we're going with you."

Hannah sighed. "Okay, then!" She hissed in frustration as she walked toward her room. "I just want to get my bag." And hopefully a few minutes to herself. Darryn's presence was overwhelming; she was scared and worried, and she hated this feeling of dread she'd been carrying around for two years.

Hopefully, a few minutes alone would help her at least get her equilibrium back.

FORTY MINUTES LATER, she and Caitlin sat waiting in the restaurant. Darryn and Don wanted to stay outside and watch who entered the restaurant.

"So, where is this guy you're supposed to meet?" asked Caitlin as she glanced at her watch again.

Hannah peered over her shoulder and scanned the faces of the other customers. The now familiar niggling feeling at the back of her neck told her something was wrong.

"I don't know. Let me check with my agent." She quickly searched for her number on her phone.

While she waited for Karen to answer, she turned around to look at the door, but the people entering the restaurant were all strangers.

Finally, Karen answered her phone.

"Karen, Hannah. I'm at the restaurant where I'm supposed to meet the photographer from last week's shoot, but he isn't here. Can you check, please?"

"Of course," Karen said calmly. "Hang on if you don't mind. I'll call him from my landline."

A few minutes later, Hannah ended the call and grabbed her bag. "Let's get out of here." She grabbed Caitlin's hand.

"What?" asked Caitlin, stunned but following her out of the restaurant.

Outside, Darryn saw them and reached them in a few strides. "What happened?" he barked and put his hands on her shoulders.

"Karen says…she phoned the photographer while I was waiting. The photographer didn't make the appointment for today. He doesn't know anything about it."

Darryn glanced around them quickly before he steered her toward the car. "We have to leave. Now." He opened the back door for her.

Inside the car, Caitlin held her close.

"We're going to get to the bottom of this. Don knows an attorney; he phoned him before we left Cape Town. He's going to contact the police and see what we can do," she crooned while stroking Hannah's hair.

"They spoke to me yesterday," Hannah said. "I said I'd contact them today, but with everything…"

"It's fine. The Paris Prefecture of Police will know what to do," Caitlin continued.

Hannah tried to listen to her sister's voice, her eyes on Darryn's broad shoulders as he steered the car skillfully through the traffic.

Her phone rang, and she answered without checking who was calling. Maybe Karen had news. Maybe she had it wrong and there was miscommunication, maybe—

"So you think you're clever?" a voice hissed in her ear. "You were supposed to meet with me alone!" The furious person at the other side of the line took a deep breath. "But remember, I know where you live, I know where your sisters live, I know where your mother—"

Rage tore through Hanna. "Listen to me, you piece of trash! You have a problem with me, you deal with me. Leave my sisters and my mother out of it!"

The next minute, brakes squealed and Darryn stopped

the car. Furious, he grabbed her phone. "White, you bastard, if I get my hands on you…"

But whoever had been on the other side had put the phone down.

"Was it White? What did he say? What did he want?" Darryn barked.

Hannah threw her arms in the air. "I don't know! It could be him—he was shouting, so I can't be sure!"

Darryn's head whipped to the front again, and he gripped the steering wheel tightly. The car moved forward again.

"What did he say?" he asked again, his eyes nearly black in the rearview mirror.

"He told me he knows where my sisters and my mother…" Hannah hiccupped, "live." She ended on a sob.

Darryn muttered a string of curses, and Don put a hand on his arm. Caitlin hugged Hannah close.

Don took out his phone and started punching in a number.

"Don, phone that attorney. We have to let the police know what's going on," Caitlin said.

"Exactly what I'm doing," he said.

"I'm calling David and Dale. They should know what's going on," Darryn announced.

Chapter Six

BACK IN HER flat, Hannah stood around, not exactly sure what to do or say next. The surge of anger had left her feeling faint and she was shivering. She'd always hated confrontations and couldn't remember ever being this angry.

Don and Darryn were both on their phones, and Caitlin was making coffee. Everything looked so normal. Except it wasn't.

She walked over to her sister, wanting to be close to her.

"Where are your bags? Surely you'll be staying with me?" she asked Caitlin.

Caitlin looked up. "Are you sure? Because Don got us a suite in the building right next to you, so we could stay there…"

"Please don't," Hannah pleaded. "I have more than enough room for you. There are three bedrooms."

There was a movement behind them, and Hannah looked over her shoulder. Darryn had finished his call and was sitting down at the kitchen counter.

"Good, because I'm also staying right here," he said.

Hannah swallowed. The very idea of Darryn staying under her roof after he'd held her and kissed her had her all worked up and confused. It had been so easy to be angry with him while he'd believed Stephen's stories, but now that everything was out in the open, now that he'd apologized— well, sort of—she wasn't sure how to behave around him.

A taciturn Darryn she could handle, but a remorseful and nice one who kept touching her was a completely different story. Add to this the fact that after all this time, he still managed to reduce her to a puddle with a mere look from his chocolate-brown eyes, and she was in trouble. Fortunately, Don and Caitlin would be close by.

"That's really not necessary, I..." she began, but Darryn's eyes darkened.

"While that bloody lunatic is still out there, I'm staying close to you, okay?"

"But why? You usually can't stand the sight of me and..."

His stood up quickly. "I think we've established that isn't the case, don't you agree?" he asked silkily, sauntering closer. "But I'm happy to demonstrate my changed attitude again if you want," he said bending his head.

Hannah stared, mesmerized, at Darryn's descending mouth, but just then Don called him. With a groan, he brushed his hand against her face before he turned away.

She exhaled slowly, her eyes on his retreating body.

"Let us be there for you, please?" Caitlin asked, her eyes twinkling.

Hannah sighed and rubbed her arms. "I don't mind you and Don staying here, but Darryn? He makes me crazy!" She groaned and hugged herself.

Caitlin cocked her head. "What exactly is going on between you and Darryn? It has always been…let's say, interesting, for lack of a better word, to watch the two of you together. He's obviously smitten with you, has been since the time you spent together two years ago. 'Fell for you' was how he put it when he talked to us about the three days you spent together."

Dumbstruck, Hannah stared at her sister for a few minutes before she shook her head. "That was two years ago. I don't think it's true any longer. He feels bad about his behavior at the time and is trying to make up for it. That's it. Remember who we're talking about—Darryn Cavallo. The guy who changes women like he changes shirts."

Caitlin cocked her head. "That doesn't tell you something?"

"It tells me he isn't interested in settling down with one woman, ever."

"I'm not so sure about that. Maybe he was trying to find another you? Why do you think—"

"Of course he wasn't," Hannah said curtly.

Caitlin stared at her. "How do you feel about him?" she asked softly.

Hannah didn't want to meet her sister's gaze.

"Hannah?" Caitlin insisted, grimacing.

Hannah looked up.

Caitlin giggled. "Hmm, thought so." She smiled and hugged Hannah. "Why don't you tell him? He knows now what really happened two years ago and—"

"No, thank you," Hannah said adamantly. "What if the next insecure guy tells him stories about me?"

"Well, according to Don, Darryn had a bad experience with a model way back, just after he started his fashion photography. This woman *did* sleep around, so you should probably give him a break, don't you think?"

"He didn't give me one two years ago!"

Caitlin chuckled. "Typical male and typical Cavallo." She touched Hannah's hand. "When they fall in love, their strong feelings tend to freak them out. Darryn looked a bit dazed when I told him that."

"He's not in love with me, he—"

"Just immediately flew across a continent to get to you when he heard what happened to Sophie. He didn't even pack. What does that tell you?"

She stared at Hannah for minutes. "He had a suitcase with him…"

"Bought everything at the airport." Caitlin smiled.

Hannah put her hand to her head. This was all way too much. She didn't want to talk about Darryn anymore. Pain was a living, breathing thing behind her eyes. Dealing with a stalker and Darryn Cavallo simultaneously had her senses in overdrive, her emotions jumbled, her usually calm demeanor in tatters.

"Where…where is Donato?" she asked, desperately hoping to change the topic.

Caitlin grinned knowingly, but she answered her question. "Grandma Rosa is thrilled to look after him. I didn't want to phone Mom before I saw you, but now that she knows what's going on, she's on her way to Rosa. Donato will have two doting grandmas around."

"What did you tell her?"

"Just the bare facts, but you know her. She's not stupid and will put two and two together."

Hannah swallowed, remembering White's threat. "I'm just glad she's on her way to Don's parents and that she's not home alone."

Caitlin rubbed her arms. "Why? You don't think he was serious when he said he knew where we all live?"

Hannah shook her head. "I don't know what he's capable of, but I'll feel better if I know Mom is not alone. That bloody creep!"

"At least we all know what's going on now. I still don't understand why you didn't tell us about the whole thing right from the start."

"The last thing I ever expected was that my all my sisters and our friend would fall for a Cavallo man!" Hannah exclaimed. "What are the chances of that happening? I was trying my best to forget about Darryn when you met Don. And at first I thought the whole thing with Stephen would blow over. And then after what happened to Zoe, it dawned on me that nobody close to me is safe. That's why I didn't even attend Dana and David's wedding. He somehow always knows where I'll be. But I didn't want to bother everyone— you were all so happy!"

"We're family, sweetie. And we've all been worried about you for a while now. We want to help. And when we're around, that idiot has to get through all of us first," Caitlin said fiercely, giving her another hug. "Why don't you go and take a long bath? We'll order in."

"Oh, hell, I haven't even thought about food—I'm a terrible host."

"You're my sister, not my host. You are not to worry about a thing. Now go take a bath and think about that gorgeous hunk of a man who can't keep his eyes off of you," Caitlin giggled.

Hannah rolled her eyes as she skirted around the two brothers who were deep in conversation. The Cavallo men were all tall, dark, and so, so sexy. The temperature in any room they were in soared noticeably. Well, that was what she'd experienced anyway.

She caught Darryn's gaze as she walked past them. His eyes darkened, and he stumbled over his words. For the second time that day, she fled to her room.

Don laughed. "Man, do you have it bad."

Those were the last words she heard before she closed her door.

DARRYN SAT STARING at the policeman from the Paris Prefecture of Police, who was listening to Hannah without batting an eye. Damn it, couldn't the guy at least look interested in her problems?

Don's attorney swore by this guy, said he was one of the best. But what the hell? He played with a pen while Hannah talked—he didn't look in the least bit interested in her problems.

None of them were French, the stalker wasn't French, and that seemed to be all the damn policeman was interested in. He had brought a colleague with him who at least made notes. Not that Darryn had much hope they would do anything about it.

He jumped up and moved so he could stand behind Hannah's chair. She was buttoning and unbuttoning her shirt's top button. She was agitated, pale, and clearly very near the end of her tether. All he wanted to do was gather her close and promise her everything would be okay.

"You have security?" the policeman asked, and Don explained about the company they were using.

"That's a good company," the policeman said as he stood. "You'll let us know if anything else happens?"

Hannah nodded.

He said goodbye, turned, and walked toward the front door.

Stunned, Darryn looked after him. "Wait just a damn

minute!" he called out and moved purposefully forward. "Is there nothing you can do in the meantime?" he nearly shouted.

Don grabbed his arm and pulled him back. "Thank you," Don said, holding on to Darryn's arm.

Darryn jerked his arm away as the policemen closed the front door behind them. "They're not going to do a thing, and you let them go?"

"Calm down," Don said, pushing Darryn down onto the closest chair. He looked over his shoulder. "You're upsetting the women, you idiot," he said softly.

Darryn threw his head back and swore softly. "I'm sorry, but..."

"Give them a chance to do their job, please?" Don said. "Didn't someone mention food?"

There was a knock on the door. Caitlin smiled as she walked toward the door. "They're just in time, it seems."

HANNAH SAT STARING at nothing in particular as Caitlin and Don unpacked the food and opened the wine. She should get up and help—it was her apartment after all. But her throat ached, her thoughts kept jumping all over the place, and it was difficult to do simple things.

She didn't have high hopes that the police would be able to do much. From what she'd experienced so far, Stephen White managed to stay hidden until he decided to strike next. And it seemed as if his bouts of anger had escalated. He had tried to push Sophie in front of an approaching car!

"Don't," Caitlin said and crouched in front of her, taking her hand. "Nothing can happen tonight. Let's try and forget about that horrible man for a few hours and relax. You need to eat, please."

With an effort, Hannah tried to smile, but she didn't think she was pulling it off. Caitlin looked worried. The bloody man was not only affecting her life; what he was doing was also a burden on her family.

"It smells wonderful," she said as she stood.

"Come and see," Caitlin smiled and pushed her toward the dining room table.

Caitlin had set the table beautifully, and Hannah swallowed against the lump in her throat. She'd missed her family. Having Caitlin here was such a comfort.

Don looked at his watch and pointed outside. "It's nine o'clock and the sun is only setting now. Shall we leave the curtains open to watch the sunset?"

"It's not going to be for a while yet, so let's leave it open. It's a beautiful evening," Hannah said as Darryn pulled a chair out for her.

As she sat down, his hand moved over her shoulders before he pressed down softly on her arm. She blinked furiously. She absolutely refused to cry just because Darryn was being nice to her!

Chapter Seven

SOMEONE PUSHED HER violently from behind, and the yellow scarf came loose as she staggered forward, trying to regain her balance. She cried out as she saw the scarf falling, falling, falling...

Hannah's eyes flew open and, scrambling upright, she covered her mouth. With shaking hands, she switched on her bedside lamp just as her door flew open.

Darryn stormed into her room shutting the door behind him. She barely had time to register that he was only wearing a pair of jeans before he was on the bed beside her and had gathered her close.

"What happened? Are you okay? Why did you cry out?" he demanded as his hands stroked unsteadily over her back.

"Bad dream," she got out, but didn't move away immediately. Her heart was beating frantically, and she wasn't sure whether it was because of the dream or because of the very sexy near-naked man holding her.

Gulping in a hysterical giggle, she pressed her face against his body. She'd just had a bad dream; she should still be in shock, not lusting after Darryn Cavallo. He pulled her head onto his shoulder.

Her hands splayed over his muscled torso and she leaned against him. It would only be for a minute. She stared at her hands. At least while touching him, they weren't shaking.

She closed her eyes. It was so good to be able to literally lean on someone. To have a physical body with her to chase away the bad dreams.

Her hands moved, exploring each hard muscle. He inhaled sharply and, beneath her fingers, his heart skipped a beat. She stilled.

"Hannah," he whispered, and she lifted her head, unable to do anything else.

He kissed her softly, his tongue gently stroking her lips, and she shuddered.

"You're killing me," he groaned, and folding his hand behind the back of her neck, pulled her closer.

HE SHOULDN'T BE doing this. She'd had a bad dream and his brother and sister-in-law were two doors down, but the moment Hannah's lips opened and she invited him into her mouth, he forgot about everything else. He finally had his arms around the woman he'd been dreaming about for two damn years.

He wanted to savor the moment, wanted to prolong their pleasure, but she was all curves and angles beneath his hands, her body moving in sync with his, and with a growl, he lifted her pajama top.

"Hannah, sweetie, are you okay?" Caitlin's voice called from the other side of the door.

Darryn heard her voice from far away, but ignored it. Hannah pushed against him, and he lifted his head.

"Hannah?" Caitlin's voice was more persistent now, and she knocked on the door.

"I'm fine!" Hannah called out.

As she slid off the bed, Darryn gulped in deep breaths. Damn it to hell! He looked down. He was in no state to get up. He looked up, finding Hannah's eyes also on his crotch. Giggling, she rushed to the door and opened it.

"I…had a bad dream, but then Darryn came—"

"Darryn is in your room?" Caitlin asked, and with a sigh, Darryn turned around so he was lying on his tummy, facing the door.

"Yes, I'm with her. You can go back to bed," he said tersely.

"Well, in that case, I'll leave you two alone," Caitlin said, her voice full of mirth.

"Thanks for checking up on me," Hannah said softly before she closed the door.

Turning around, her hands still behind her, she locked the door. He'd barely registered the locking bit when she lifted her pajama top over her head. Walking toward him with those long legs of hers, her blue eyes dark, deep pools of navy, she let the top slide down her arm until it dropped to the ground.

Without taking his eyes off of her, he edged closer to the side of the bed. She moved closer and shimmied out of her very short, very sexy pajama bottoms, which fell to the floor. She stepped out of them and moved between his legs with one movement.

He'd stopped thinking when she locked the door. Feeling had taken over his mind and his body. His hands moved without a message from his brain and glided down her sides. Her flesh was smooth, hot, irresistible.

She pushed him and he fell backward, watching as she crawled over him, her glorious long, blonde hair tumbling forward. He remembered this from before, was his last rational thought.

This time, she kissed him, plunging her tongue into his wet, waiting mouth. His fingers got lost in her hair as he swallowed her soft moans. But he wanted, needed more. With a quick flip, he reversed their positions so she was lying underneath him.

Reverently, his hands followed the contours of her body, down her sides and then back up. Satin and velvet, slopes and curves—she was irresistible. He tried to keep a tight rein on himself; he could devour the whole of her. But she was vulnerable, shook up, and he had to at least try to be civilized.

Her breath was coming in short gasps, her body stretching and bending beneath his touch. He watched her as he touched her breast.

"Darryn," She gasped.

"I'm here," he crooned and bent his head, needing desperately to taste her skin. Time stood still as he teased, caressed, and loved every sexy centimeter of her body with his hands and mouth until the heat radiating from beneath her skin was almost scorching him.

When he cupped her heat, she bucked beneath his hand and muttered his name over and over again as she let go.

After long minutes, Hannah opened her eyes to find Darryn staring down at her.

"That was the most beautiful thing I've ever seen," he murmured and bent down to catch her lips with his again.

And immediately the heat, the hunger, the longing to be a part of her, was back. But it seemed this time she was bent on making him lose control. She smiled slyly, turned her body quickly, and had him on his back again so she could straddle him.

He grinned wickedly. "Oh, so you want to be on top?"

"Yeah, I do. Besides, I have to take these off." She started pulling at his jeans. "You are wearing way too many clothes."

He lifted himself so she could pull his jeans down.

Her eyes widened as she pushed and pulled. "No briefs?" she asked breathlessly as her hands grazed him in the process.

He moaned, quickly kicking the pants away. "Come here. Enough torture for now." He pulled her up so she was lying on top of him. He looked down at their bodies as his hands stroked down her back. "Look at us," he muttered. "You are a perfect fit—we were made for each other."

She caught her breath and stared down at him.

A tear escaped and rolled down her cheek.

"I love you," she said brokenly, touching his face. "I've always loved you."

For a minute Darryn thought his heart would explode. Hugging her close to him, he whispered her name over and over again.

"It's okay, you don't have to say it. I know you don't feel the same way and it's—" she said, but when he registered what she was saying, he cursed and sat up quickly.

He had both arms around her to make sure she didn't move before he had his say. "Damn it to hell, Hannah. How can you say that?" he snapped. "Look at us! We're both naked and I'm in your bed!" He shook her gently. "Two years ago I lost my heart to you, and however hard I tried, I've never been able to get it back. It belongs to you—always will. Because," he said, cupping her face, "I love you. You've touched my very depths, and no one else will ever do for me but you."

"But you have a different woman on your arm every—"

He kissed her. It seemed to be one sure way of shutting her up. He really only meant for it be a quick kiss, so she would stop talking nonsense, but the moment he tasted her and her lips moved under his, he was lost.

"It's only ever been you," he murmured, before he lifted

her up so he could become a part of her.

She gasped as he pushed into her. Her eyes opened, and she started moving with him. It had always been like this. It was if she knew what he wanted and moved with him as if they were one.

"I love you," he said as he increased the rhythm. He tried to watch her, tried to stay focused, but his senses spun into overdrive, spiraling him out of control.

Chapter Eight

SOMETHING HAD WOKEN her up. It was still dark outside, and behind her, Darryn was still asleep, breathing deeply. Her cell phone was lit up. She was used to getting messages at all hours of the day; it was probably Karen. Carefully, Hannah lifted Darryn's arm that was holding her against him and slipped from the bed. She had to go to the bathroom anyway and would see what Karen wanted.

In the bathroom, she washed her face and stared at herself in the mirror—she looked thoroughly loved. Groaning, she dried her face. She shouldn't be awake. They'd hardly slept. She blushed and put her hands to her flaming face. Wow, the man had moves and then some. When she remembered all the things she'd done to him, what he'd done to her, her pulse picked up and she had difficulty breathing.

Phone. That was why she was here. She had to check her messages. She clicked on her phone and the text message jumped out at her. Her legs gave way, and she sank to the floor. No, no, no! Grabbing her mouth to prevent a sob escaping, she put her head on her knees.

The message was from Stephen White.

Although his name didn't appear anywhere, she knew it was from him.

So you think having your family around you and a Cavallo in your bed will keep me away? GET RID OF THE SECURITY GUARD AND GET AWAY FROM CAVALLO OR I WILL KILL HIM!!!

And below the horrible words were two pictures—one from the four of them when they were having dinner and one of Darryn on her bed. She hadn't closed the windows, she remembered.

Hannah lifted her head and wiped her cheeks. This was never going to be over; he was never going to stop, and there wasn't anyone who could do anything about it. The only way she could protect those near and dear to her was to do what she'd been doing—keep as far away from them as possible. But this time, she would have to disappear as well. At least for a while.

For a minute, she considered telling Darryn about the threat. Maybe she could persuade him to disappear with her, maybe they could... With a sob, her face fell into her hands. Darryn would never back away from someone like Stephen White, and if anything happened to him, it would kill her. This was something she would have to do on her own.

Her mind made up, she got up unsteadily while her brain worked overtime. She'd phone Karen when she was on the move. Before the others woke up, she'd have to be gone. None of them would back away if she were to tell them about Stephen's message, and she needed to know they'd be safe.

She grabbed her toiletries bag. This was all that she would take with her. Whatever else she needed, she could buy or get from her apartment in Cape Town. Her handbag with her passport and cards was on her dressing table. If her luck held, Darryn wouldn't wake up. Her phone. She'd have to get rid of that. But first she'd send everyone a message. It would be easy enough to get a new phone at the airport and hopefully it would take a while before Stephen had the new number.

Nobody had to be able find her.

And the security guard? She'd have to think of something quickly.

DARRYN OPENED HIS eyes and he knew—Hannah was gone. The sun was up; a light breeze blew in from the open window. He looked around. Everything looked the same as it did last night, not that he could remember much, he only had eyes for Hannah. But she wasn't there.

An emptiness filled his being. His phone bleeped. Grabbing it, he sat up. For a long time he simply stared at the message. A sharp knife went right through his side, pierced his heart and left it bleeding. Hannah had indeed left.

Forget about last night, it shouldn't have happened, she wrote. She was fine; she needed to be alone. He had to get on with his life and forget about her. He reread her words three more times, but the message stayed the same—she had left, she didn't want to be with him.

Swearing, he grabbed his jeans and, jumping around, finally got them on. A look inside her closets told him she hadn't taken anything with her.

For a minute, he leaned against the wall, his heart breaking into a million little pieces. This time the hurt cut deeper. After last night, he'd thought she'd trusted him. Hadn't she told him she loved him? And hadn't he told her the same thing? Added foolishly that his heart was hers? But she'd left, so last night obviously meant nothing to her.

Still stunned, he opened the door and walked into the corridor. Caitlin was standing right outside the bedroom in which she and Don had slept, looking dazed.

"Did you get a message from Hannah?" she whispered through dry lips.

"Yep," he said, walking past her to the room in which he should have stayed last night.

But Caitlin grabbed his arm and stopped him. "What did she say?" she asked anxiously.

He barked out a laugh. "That last night was a mistake, she's leaving, I have to get on with my life." He made a big deal of looking at his phone again. "That's it, more or less. That's what she wants, and I, for one, am quite happy to give her exactly what she is asking for. I'm leaving as soon as the plane is ready. Let me know if you and Don want to go with me."

Caitlin stared at him for a few minutes. "In her message to me she said she 'has' to go. I'm sure Stephen White is behind this and—"

"We're here, there is a security guard at the front door, this is the safest place for her!" He pushed his fingers through his hair and then dropped his hand to his side, feeling deflated. "She told me she loved me," he said softly. "And bloody fool that I was, I told her the same. This…running away, sending me a damn text message, telling me to get on with my life after last night, I…" He struggled to breathe and inhaled deeply. "I should've stayed the hell away from her."

He turned his back to Caitlin and stepped into his room, closing the door behind him. He had to call to make sure the plane was ready; he wanted to leave as soon as possible.

Ten minutes later, he walked into the kitchen, his bag in his hand.

"You're really leaving?" Caitlin asked coldly.

"What the hell do you want from me?" he nearly yelled.

His heart had splintered into a million pieces—what else was he supposed to do?

"I want you to be there for her, you idiot! I want you to stop thinking about Darryn Cavallo for one minute and to think why Hannah is gone. It's not something she would do. And if you really loved her, you would know that."

Don gave him a cool look and took his wife into his

arms. "You've upset my wife," he said, his eyes chips of ice.

"I—" Darryn rubbed his face. "I'm leaving. Are you coming with me?"

"No, we're staying another day. Just in case. Caitlin has been on the phone, trying to find out whether anyone else knows something about Hannah. Her agent also received a message from Hannah saying she'll get in touch with her soon." Don grimaced. "And she duped the security guy into checking the dining room window while she slipped away. So he also doesn't know anything about her movements."

Darryn wanted to explode. "Bloody hell! We've put our lives on hold to rush to her side and she does a disappearing act after one day? I'm out of here!"

Caitlin stepped out of Don's arms. "Something isn't right. Hannah would never do something like this. I still think something must have happened and that Stephen White has a hand in the whole thing."

"Whatever. I've called the airport. I'm leaving. See you back home," he snarled and stormed out of Hannah's flat.

Images of the night they spent together clouded his mind, driving him insane. She had been a willing and enthusiastic lover—they couldn't get enough of each other. He'd fallen asleep once or twice only to be woken by butterfly kisses over his face and body, and that was all it took to rekindle the fire that had nearly consumed them.

He had explored and loved every centimeter of her body, leaving them both satisfied time after time. Hell, he thought they would pick up where they left off, when they finally fell asleep. But she had slipped away while he was sleeping, without saying a word.

This only reminded him of his rule—never sleep over. It was a rule he'd broken only twice in his life, and both times it was because of Hannah Sutherland.

Well, he was done with her for good. His heart simply wouldn't be able to take another blow.

He tried to hold on to his anger and his hurt all through the eleven-hour flight home. Sleep was impossible, he couldn't eat, and his stomach was tied up in knots. He downed a beer, paced the small aircraft.

And somewhere over Africa, his brain started functioning again, and he was able to think.

Caitlin's words kept bothering him—it wasn't something Hannah would do. And if he really loved her, he would know that. Again, he saw Hannah's sleek, sexy body rising above him, teasing him, driving him slowly insane until he became a part of her.

Was it possible he had it wrong? But where the hell was Hannah? Why had she left so abruptly? Had something happened? Why the hell didn't she tell him about it? Worry clawed at his insides and, frustrated and feeling powerless, he eventually sat down in a chair.

Rubbing his face, he tried to think. Had he said or done something that could have her had her running away? Surely after last night, she had to know how he felt about her. He'd loved her the whole night long—with his body, with his soul, with his very being—and she had been with him every step of the way. So what the hell spooked her?

He rubbed his chest. Breathing was difficult. Hell, he never knew missing someone could cause a physical pain, but that was what he was experiencing.

HANNAH HAD DITCHED her normal smart, casual look for jeans and running shoes and had bundled her hair in a cap. The biggest pair of sunglasses she could find covered most of her face. This wouldn't stop Stephen from recognizing her, but hopefully she could reach South Africa before he realized she was gone.

As she walked toward the plane, she looked surreptitiously around her, but there was no sign of the telltale prickling on the back of her neck that always warned her when Stephen was around, and she was praying she would be able to get on the plane without anybody finding out.

She'd been racking her brain trying to think of a place where she could hide when she found a brochure in her handbag about Jacobsbaai, a tiny village on the west coast of the Western Cape in South Africa. She had been there for a shoot about a year ago and had fallen in love with the quiet, pretty little village with its whitewashed houses, dirt roads, and cobalt blue sea.

Somewhere close to the sea, that was where she wanted

to be. She had been away from a beach and the ocean for far too long.

A phone call later, she'd booked the holiday house she'd stayed in before. It was a big house, and although it was possible for her to rent only the loft part of the house, she wanted to be alone and had taken the whole place. She had to think, had to make a plan to make sure Stephen didn't hurt those she loved.

Nobody could know she was back in South Africa, even though everything inside of her urged her to phone her mother. Darryn would find out and she wanted to make sure he stayed as far away from her as possible. Just the possibility that something could happen to him because of her had her breaking out in a cold sweat.

She rented a car at the airport to drive to Jacobsbaai so she wouldn't have to use her own car. Stephen was bound to know her license plate...he seemed to know everything. She'd also taken all the cash from the safe in her flat in Paris. Credit cards could be traced and Stephen seemed to know exactly what she was doing every minute of every day.

Chapter Nine

WHEN DARRYN GOT off the plane in Cape Town late that evening, his two other brothers were waiting for him.

Damn it to hell and back. He had a hole inside him the size of the wide open spaces of the Great Karoo, his head wanted to explode trying to figure out where the hell Hannah could be, and now he had to face the inquisition!

He glared at them as he walked closer. "What are you doing here?"

"We have news," David said. "But let's get to Rosa's; everyone else is there guarding the phone."

"I'm not interested in any news, thank you. I'm going home." He grunted, trying to walk around them.

David grabbed his arm. "Will you stop being an ass and come with us?" his normally mild brother barked out.

"You're upset, we all are. Hannah is one of us and she's in trouble," Dale added. "Let's go."

Seething with resentment, frustration, and anger, Darryn followed them. He wanted to punch something, and his brothers looked like good targets at the moment.

"I'm sick with worry, don't you get it? Why the hell did she leave without saying anything to me? When I heard she was in danger, I flew over a bloody continent to get to her, and what does she do? She bolts. Damnit, what am I supposed to think?" he spat out.

Dale slapped him on the back. "Maybe you should start your sentences with Hannah and not 'I'—might help you lose those blinders you have on."

Darryn ground his teeth as they neared David's car.

"I have my own car here," he mumbled.

"You go with David, I'll drive your car," Dale said. He held out his hand "Keys."

"I can drive my own damn car!" Darryn said as he took out his keys.

"Get in and shut up." David growled. "Save your breath for later—you have to explain to her sisters and mother why you couldn't wait to leave Paris."

"I—" Darryn began hotly.

Dale grabbed his keys. "There's that 'I' again," he said mildly. "Where is your car?"

"That's right," Darryn said, "because I'm the one—"

"Where did you park your car?" Dale asked again.

"I—"

"Tell Dale and get in the damn car. We're wasting time," David snarled and started the car.

Cussing, Darryn got in. Bloody hell, nobody seemed to be interested in how he was feeling. He wasn't the one who walked away!

It was quiet in the car all the way to his mother's restaurant. When David stopped the car, Dale parked right behind him, and the two of them got out of the cars without a word and walked to the front door, leaving Darryn still sitting in the car.

Before he even opened the car door, they'd disappeared inside.

Reluctantly, he got out and closed the car door behind him. The last thing he wanted to do at this point was to talk to his family, but it seemed he had no choice in the matter.

As he started toward the restaurant, Brenda, Hannah's mom, appeared in the doorway. Her eyes were red; it was clear she had been crying. And just like that, the last of his anger faded.

Hannah's mother rushed to his side. "I know you're angry with Hannah, but please come in and listen, we've heard something, and we're trying to figure out what it means," she said, her eyes glistening with tears, her lip quivering.

He hugged her. Damn, he couldn't stand anyone crying.

"I'll listen," he said after clearing his throat.

Everyone was waiting inside. It was late; the waiters were cleaning the last of the tables.

His mother was the only one with a welcoming smile. "Sweetheart," she crooned and hugged him.

She stared up into his face for long minutes. "You love Hannah. We all know that."

Surprised, he took a step back. "How did you know? Oh, Don probably told you."

His mother smiled. "It has been so obvious to all of us how you feel about her. We were only waiting for you to acknowledge it."

Brenda clapped her hands and smiled through her tears. Darryn grimaced. Hannah's mother was always looking for the next real-life love story.

"I knew it! And Hannah loves you?" she asked breathlessly.

"That's what she said, but then she—" Darryn began, but Brenda stopped him with a touch on his arm.

"Hannah never stops talking about you. Of course, she never says anything nice, but that's what alerted me to the fact she has feelings for you. And, Darryn, she has never told any man that."

His mother touched his face. "And you're hurting because she left you. I understand that. But—"

Zoe stormed forward, interrupting his mother, and punched him on the shoulder. "But if you love her, you should know she would never walk away without a good reason!"

He rubbed his shoulder. Damn, the woman packed quite a punch. He looked up to see Dale's eyes twinkling. His brother was obviously pleased his wife had managed to do something he had probably been thinking about doing as well.

Dana moved toward him with purposeful strides, and he backed up a few steps, holding up his hands. "Okay!" he called out. "Sheez! I'm here. I'll listen to your news but don't expect me to be happy about it," he snarled.

Dana pressed a finger against his shoulder. "You're an idiot. We all love you, but I don't much like you at this point," she said coldly before turning back into David's arms.

His dad slapped him on the back. Hard.

Wincing, he turned around.

"Damnit, stop slapping me. I'm hurt badly enough. I get it! You're all mad at me because I left Hannah's flat. But, damnit, why the hell did she leave? We spent the whole night together. I told her I love her, but when I opened my eyes, she was gone. What the hell else was I supposed to do?"

"Trust her and find out why she left," his dad said succinctly and put his hand on his shoulder. "Sit down and listen. Don phoned about an hour ago. Because he didn't run away like some people," he said nearly crushing Darryn's shoulder, "he has been able to pull a few strings, call in favors, and had people scouring airports in all the major cities in France and the neighboring countries. As a result, we now know that Hannah boarded a plane from Paris to Cape Town, and Stephen White got on a plane heading for Cape Town from Brussels. Don and Caitlin are also on their way."

Stunned, Darryn stared at his father. It took him a few

minutes to digest his dad's words. He shook his head. Did that mean…? Thousands of chaotic thoughts bounced around in his head—what if? *Is it possible?* But why would… And then he finally realized what his dad's words implied.

"She's here, in South Africa, and he found out and followed her," he whispered through dry lips. "But why didn't she say anything?"

"For the same reason she missed most of our family gatherings over the last few months," David said and pulled Zoe closer. "The same reason she hasn't been back home, or hardly made any contact with her sisters—because…" He paused dramatically, holding his one hand in the air.

"She's worried he may hurt someone else," Darryn finished his sentence.

Everyone else started talking. Darryn fell back against the chair. The roaring in his ears made it difficult to assimilate what he'd just heard. But finally, all the pieces of the puzzle fell into place, and he jumped up.

"I'm going to wring her bloody neck," he vowed fervently. "What the hell was she thinking?"

"What she's always thinking about—other people. She'll do anything to make sure no one else gets hurt. My Hannah is a caretaker, a nurturer—she simply can't help the way she reacts," Brenda said softly.

"So where is she?" Darryn asked and looked around the room.

Zoe shook her head. "We've been racking our brains, but

I don't know! She's not answering her phone; we knocked on the door of her apartment in Sea Point, Cape Town, but no one answered. Caitlin has a key, so we'll take a look when she arrives. Hannah didn't contact any of us, not even Mom, and that is so not her! She must be frightened out of her mind," she ended on a sob. Dale pulled her close to him.

Darryn stared at Zoe while her words sank in.

She was somewhere in the country, but they didn't know where.

There was silence for long minutes. Frustrated, Darryn started pacing. Where could she be? He tried to remember the names of places she had spoken about, but he realized quickly they didn't talk much when they were together. They either tried to avoid each other, or they made love.

He knew so little about her. When Caitlin told him Hannah gave money to a fund for war orphans, it came as a surprise. But considering everything else he'd heard about Hannah over the last twenty-four hours, it now made complete sense. He had been the idiot who only saw her beautiful face, enjoyed her body, but never bothered to really get to know her.

"At least if we can't find her, chances are White won't be able to either," David said into the silence.

"But we have to find her before he does," Brenda said, her eyes brimming with tears again.

Darryn pulled the older woman into his arms. "We will. I promise," he said, and a strange calmness came over him.

"What about the police?" he asked his brothers, although he knew the answer.

"We'll do better using a private detective; as we all know, our police are completely useless," David said. "However we should probably contact them as well, just to have our fears on record. And maybe, you never know, there might just be a lone policeman or woman who will actually do something."

Darryn nodded. Unfortunately, it was so true. The last two chiefs of police were in jail. He wouldn't put too much hope on the police. They would have to rely on a private company and themselves. Because they had to find Hannah. He loved her; he needed her. Around her, he became a better version of himself.

"Is there anything you can tell us about White that might help us?" Hannah's mother asked.

"Wait a minute," his mother said. "White. Stephen White. I only now register his name. Is this the little guy who went to school with you?" his mother asked.

"Yeah, but we were never friends. How come you remember him?" Darryn asked.

"I remember his mother. She was always going on about how he worshiped you and tried to imitate everything you did. He even started playing rugby, because you were captain of the first rugby team."

Darryn stared at her. "He contacted me when I was a fashion photographer."

"He wanted to do what you were doing," his mother said.

Don swore. "So when you got to be with Hannah…"

Darryn shook his head. "Damn, I never knew that, Mom. He was so into computers, I was surprised when he contacted me about photography."

"So his computer skills must be how he always knows Hannah's whereabouts," Don said. "And she undoubtedly figured that out as well, which is why we can't get hold of her. She probably got rid of her phone."

"So what you're telling me is that he is capable of hacking into any system, including ours?" David asked incredulously.

"That's the problem. I'm not sure what he's capable of. All I know is that we have to get to Hannah before he figures out where she is."

"It's late—we're not going to get anything else done tonight," his mother said while getting up. "Don and Caitlin will be back tomorrow; let's meet at their place over lunch."

"I'll make a list of places Hannah spoke about," Zoe added.

"I'll see what I can find out about getting a private detective," David said. "I have contacts."

"Maybe she will still contact one of us," Brenda said.

Darryn hugged her close, needing her warmth as much as she needed the hug.

Chapter Ten

HANNAH OPENED HER eyes and lay listening to the waves crashing against the rocks. The house here at Jacobsbaai was close to the sea, and the noise was deafening. But she loved it.

Ever since she was a little girl, the sea had called out to her. Everything about it enchanted her—the color, the movement, the unpredictability, the power, the gentleness, the smell, the touch of the water against her skin. As a little girl, she'd sometimes wondered if she was a mermaid. Her mother used to tease her and said she could swim before she could walk.

She wished Darryn could be here with her. They would have a breakfast picnic on the beach, swim later on, and would come back here to make love…

Jumping up, she wiped her eyes. Thinking about what she couldn't have was not helping. The bigger the distance between her and Darryn, the safer he would be. Something had to happen; she couldn't go on like this.

But for now, she was going for a swim. She rummaged through her suitcase to find her wet suit. It was one of the items she got from her apartment in Sea Point. She figured she had about half a day before Stephen White would realize she'd left Paris, so she took the chance to go to her apartment to pack extra clothes.

She hated the fact she couldn't contact any of her sisters or her mother, but she didn't want to take the chance Stephen had somehow gotten hold of the number of her new phone. She had no idea what he was capable of doing.

The water of the Atlantic was freezing, even in summer, and this time of year it would be very cold. But that wasn't going to deter her from spending time in the waves.

Coffee would have to wait until she got back.

The sea was calling her. Minutes later, she crashed into the first wave. The cold knocked the breath out of her, and she laughed. There was no one else on the beach and, for the first time in a long time, she was able to relax.

Turning her back on the sea, she looked out over the tiny village. At least if Stephen bloody White came for her, she would see him coming.

Her headache was gone this morning, and she could think more clearly. Somehow, over the course of the day, she would have to come up with some sort of plan.

She turned around and dove under the next wave.

And she had to find a way to not think of Darryn every single second. But after the night they'd spent together, she didn't know how that would be possible.

He would probably never speak to her again after her

disappearing act. But that was fine. At least he was safe.

"She'll be somewhere close to the sea," Hannah's mother said.

"She's been to her apartment; Zoe and I went there early this morning. Her flat is neat as usual, but there were telltale signs she was there very recently. Her mailbox is empty, for one."

They were all sitting around Caitlin and Don's dining room table and making a list of places Hannah might have gone.

"She won't go to Hermanus, because you live there, Mom. And she is keeping far away from us," Zoe said.

Dana sat forward. "Her agent knows about Stephen White, by the way. I called her this morning. I was wondering how she would get in touch with Hannah, and she said Hannah had promised to call her once a week. She'll let me know when she hears from her."

Caitlin got up. "I thought of calling her friends, but I'm worried some of them may know this Stephen guy. I've also realized she will stay away from everyone she knows, because she's afraid he'll hurt them." She inhaled on a shudder and put her face in her hands. "I can't believe this is happening, to Hannah of all people," she ended with a sob.

Don pulled her into his arms. "We'll find her, sweetheart, we'll find her," he soothed her. Tucking his wife close to him, he looked at his mother-in-law. "So, Brenda, you think she'll choose to be close to the sea. We've established that she didn't fly to Johannesburg." He pointed at Zoe. "And Zoe doesn't think she'll go to Hermanus. She could, of course, have gone to one of the smaller towns on the other side of Hermanus or even to one of the other suburbs in Cape Town, but if she wants to stay far away from us, I don't think so. So that leaves…"

"The West Coast," Darryn exclaimed and, pushing his chair back, got up. For the first time since they started talking, he had a glimmer of hope that they might find out where Hannah was hiding. "Any particular place you think she may be?" he asked, looking at Zoe and Caitlin.

They were both frowning, obviously trying to think of something.

"Hannah didn't talk much about her work over the last two years, and we've all been so busy falling in love and getting married, and though we all knew something was wrong, we didn't insist she tells us." Zoe sighed. "We're wasting time. Let's have a look at a map, divide the West Coast into parts, and start phoning every single hotel and bed and breakfast."

"Why don't you ladies let us handle this?" Don asked.

Darryn held his breath. What he knew of women, especially the women around this table, told him they were not going to accept Don's suggestion without a fight.

But to his amazement, they all looked at one another and

nodded.

"Whatever you feel is best, my dear," his mother said.

He didn't quite trust the light in her eyes, but before he could say anything, she cast her eyes downward.

"Great." Don smiled. "Come on guys, let's go to my study so we can begin."

IT WAS LATE when Darryn stopped in front of his house in Camp's Bay. He pressed the remote and the gate opened noiselessly. He drove in, his mind on Hannah. Where the hell was she?

With his brothers' help, they'd gotten hold of a map of the West Coast and had phoned every single bed and breakfast and hotel from Yzerfontein up the coast to Lambert's Bay. Nothing. Nobody had a booking under her name or someone with her description.

He was going to look for more maps tonight. Maybe there was a small town they'd missed, one that wasn't on the map they were using.

The garage doors opened, and he drove inside.

This was ridiculous, damn it. He simply couldn't spend another day sitting around and calling people. Tomorrow he was going to drive up the West Coast, and even if it took him weeks, he would bloody well find her.

He got out and slammed the door behind him. First things first. He had to get hold of another map. As he closed the door that led from the garage to the kitchen behind him, he activated the silent alarms outside his house like he always did.

Minutes later, he was staring at another map on his computer. This one was more detailed, and he found three little towns he didn't remember seeing on the other map.

He took out his phone and, walking toward the big windows overlooking the sea, he sent his brothers a message, listing the towns they'd missed. Tonight he'd find the telephone numbers of accommodations in the towns and, while driving tomorrow, he could start calling.

The hairs on his neck rose when he noticed the red light beneath the kitchen counter flickering. He wasn't alone. Damn it, living in South Africa meant one should always be aware of what was going on around them, but he had been so distracted, he didn't do what he usually did—made sure nobody was around when he opened his gate.

He swung around, but he was too late. Stephen White was behind him, his face contorted in rage. He was holding some kind of stick above his head with both hands. Darryn stared, not quite believing what was in front of him. The next minute, White brought down his hands.

Darryn tried to jump aside, his foot caught on something, and he started to fall backward as White tried to hit him. The blow just missed him. The sound of approaching sirens grew. Hopefully, it was the security people reacting to the silent alarm.

"She's mine," White yelled, lifting his arms again. "I saw her first—this time I'm going to be the winner!"

Darryn scurried back. White's arms came down again; the blow barely missed his head, but landed on his shoulder. He tried to get up and stay focused.

"I could have had her, but then you came along!" White yelled, and with a maniacal smile, he swung the stick and brought it down again.

Pain exploded in Darryn's head, and blackness mercifully engulfed him.

HE WAS SWIMMING in a sea of unbearable pain.

Voices. Were they in his head or…

Darryn tried to open his eyes but it hurt, so he kept them closed. It was cold, and he was lying on the floor. What…

"Mr. Cavallo?"

He grunted and opened one eye. A few security guards were standing around him. "What happened?"

"Looks like you were attacked, sir. When we unlocked your front door, someone fled through the sliding doors," one said and pointed toward the open sliding doors.

"Can we call a doctor? The police?" another one asked.

Darryn started to shake his head, but the pain was so bad, he gasped and tried to sit up. "Just my brother…his number is on my phone. Don…" A wave of nausea forced him to stay down.

And then everything came crashing down as he remembered. Hannah. Stephen White. The bastard had been here. He was the one who'd hit him, and he was going to hurt Hannah.

"Let's get you on the couch, sir," one of the guys said, and they both grabbed his arms. He did his best to assist them, but the pain was excruciating—his shoulder, his head, his whole body ached.

Damn it, he felt ridiculously weak. He sat down slowly on the couch and leaned back against the cushions. The blackness threatened to engulf him again, nausea rose up in his throat, but he swallowed it back.

One security guard was on his phone, probably talking to Don. Why the hell was he talking so much? All he had to do was tell Don what happened. They had to go after White. That bloody coward wasn't getting away with this. Not while Darryn was still breathing.

"Sir?" the security guard said. "Your brother wants to talk to you."

Finally. "Thanks," he said and took the phone.

"What happened?" Don's asked obviously concerned.

"White. The bastard—" This time, the blackness didn't abate, but engulfed him, and the last thing he was aware of was the phone slipping from his fingers.

Chapter Eleven

TRY AS SHE might, Hannah couldn't fall asleep.

She'd been fine all through the day and never once felt unsafe. She had read a little, watched television, and thought she would fall asleep quickly like she did last night.

But now she was restless, as if something was about to happen. Not knowing whether the rest of her family was safe was driving her crazy. Coming to a decision, she put on the light and reached for her phone. It was nearly midnight, but she had to speak to her agent now. Fortunately, Karen was a night owl and seldom went to sleep before the early morning hours.

If anything had happened to anyone, they would have contacted Karen. She was sure of it. Her sisters and mother all had her agent's telephone number.

Karen answered on the first ring.

"Karen. It's Hannah."

"Hannah, sweetheart!" she called out. "I'm so glad to hear from you. Listen…"

"My family—have you heard anything from them…"

"You have to call them, Hannah."

A cold hand clutched at her trachea, forcing out most of the air. "Why? Did something happen to one of them?"

"Your mother and sisters are fine, it's just… Please call them."

Hysteria bubbled up, and Hannah breathed in deeply. "Is it Darryn? Has something happened to Darryn?"

"Yes, but he's fine now, please phone them," Karen insisted. "I'm going to put the phone down. Please get yourself a new phone. White is apparently capable of hacking into any system." The next minute the line went dead.

Stunned, Hannah sat for a few seconds before she got up. An icy calm settled over her. Darryn had been hurt by Stephen. He wanted a reaction? Well, he'd get one. She was mad as hell and finished being the victim.

She grabbed her bag and flung her clothes in haphazardly. Fortunately, she hadn't brought much with her, so packing went quickly. She stared at her phone then dropped it in the garbage pail. Karen was right, she should leave it and get another one. Where to get another one was a problem, the little village only had the bare basics. She'd make a plan somehow to get a message to her family.

She would leave the groceries she'd bought here. She quickly messaged the owner and said she'd pay whatever they needed for someone to clean the place and she would drop the key off at her place.

Then, grabbing her keys and bag, she left the house and sprinted to her car.

All she could think of was getting to Darryn as soon as possible. But first she had to leave the key.

She looked back over her shoulder to the house as she drove away. Damn, she'd left the bedroom light on, but she'd let the landlady know. She was not turning around. Getting to Darryn was her only concern at the moment.

As she stopped in front of the landlady's house, the porch light came on, and the woman appeared in the doorway. Hannah sighed. She had hoped she could just drop the key in the mailbox. Getting out and talking to the landlady would mean wasting more time, but she couldn't just drive away now.

She met the woman at the gate. "I'm sorry, I didn't want to disturb you. And I'm so sorry to have to leave so early, but I have a…a family emergency," she said as she handed over the keys.

"You've paid for a whole month!" the woman exclaimed. "I—"

"I'll come back on another date and will call you, if that's all right?" she said. "Which reminds me. I've misplaced my cell phone and want to let my sister Caitlin know I'm on my way. Could I please ask you to send her a message?"

"Of course," she said, "I have my phone in my pocket." She gave Hannah her phone. "Put in her number, and I'll send the message."

Hannah quickly entered the number, told the woman about the light that was still on, and thanked her before she jogged back to the car. She'd filled up the tank when she'd arrived, so fortunately, she didn't have to make another stop right now.

WHEN DARRYN NEXT opened his eyes, his three brothers and Hank, a doctor friend of Dale's he'd met before, were staring down at him, all frowning. He groaned and looked around. He was in his bed. A damn good thing, given the ringing in his ears. The pain pounding away behind his eyes was driving him crazy.

"What are you all doing here, and how did I get into bed? What time is it?" he groaned.

"It's half past one. I spoke to you on the phone, remember? Or tried to, but you passed out. So I had no choice, I had to call in the troops, so we could come and save your sorry ass," Don teased. "Also your sisters-in-law threatened to come if we didn't. What the hell happened?"

"It was White," Darryn said and touched his head. He winced as he touched bandages covering the side of his head. "He hit me with a bat or something. First on my shoulder and then against my head. What the hell is this?"

"There is a lump on your head the size of a golf ball," Dale snickered, relief replacing the anxiousness of moments ago on his face. "Hank had to do something."

Hank handed him some pills. "For the pain. You have a concussion, and I'll feel better if we can move you to a hospital, you—"

"Forget about it," Darryn interjected, but he swallowed the painkillers.

"Told you," Dale said, smiling.

"You should stay in bed, then, and come see me when you get up. I'd like to take an X-ray of your shoulder," Hank insisted.

Darryn nodded.

"How did White get in here?" Dale asked. "You have security all around your place."

"I don't know. I didn't look around when I opened the gate like I usually do, because I was distracted. I don't know whether he slipped in then or whether he'd somehow climbed over the fence—I wouldn't put anything past that creep. Anyway, he triggered the silent alarm, but by the time I saw the flickering light, he was already behind me. Damned man. Next time I see him, I'll…" He tried to sit upright, but a wave of nausea had him leaning back against the pillows.

"Yeah, you're a real Rambo." Don chuckled, but he couldn't hide the worry lines on his forehead.

"He took my phone—that was the main reason I called you," Darryn remembered. "I'd just messaged you guys with the names of three other small towns we missed the first time round and—"

"She was in Jacobsbaai," David said.

"What?" This time Darryn managed to sit upright, although the world tilted scarily around him.

Don scratched his head. "Caitlin and the other women figured out that she was in Jacobsbaai, but before—"

"You see, they didn't listen to Don here when he sent them to the kitchen." David snickered.

"I didn't send anyone to the kitchen, damnit, I just didn't think—"

"They could do anything." David slapped Don on the back. "It's time we all realize—the women we married are not the kind who sit quietly in the kitchen. They take action."

"Before what?" Darryn asked, trying his best to get the conversation back to what was important.

"Before they could leave... That was their plan—to leave us behind and go and find Hannah themselves."

"You shouldn't have sent them to the kitchen." David grinned.

"Damn it, stop saying that. Get on with it, man!" Darryn said, upset and worried. He felt helpless, lying there, his head pounding, his whole body aching.

Don launched into a long description of who said what until Darryn's head was spinning. Don's last words took a while to register.

"So, what you're saying is that Hannah is on her way, but she doesn't have a phone, and we can't reach her?"

"That's about right," Don agreed.

"So where the hell is she?" Darryn demanded.

"We're not exactly sure when she left, but she could be

here any minute now," Don said.

"So, she's driving through the night while that maniac is on the loose?" Darryn bellowed and winced as pain nearly blinded him.

"If you don't calm down, we're dragging you to the hospital," Hank cautioned him.

"Just get her here, please?" he asked before dizziness and fatigue forced him to close his eyes again.

HOW EXACTLY SHE finally reached Darryn's house, Hannah wasn't sure. She kept her eyes on the white line of the road, her foot on the pedal, and she drove. Anger kept her wide awake throughout the ninety-minute drive. She made one stop to put in more gas, but she hadn't even gotten out of the car.

She'd left Darryn after spending an incredible night with him, had left her sister, hadn't contacted any friends or anyone else in her family to make sure they would be all safe. And what did the bastard do? He attacked Darryn—the love of her life, in spite of everything.

So she was done playing nice. It was time to confront this creep. If he wanted her, then that was what he'd get. She didn't often get angry, but this had gone on long enough. How many people had to get hurt because this guy was out of control? It was going to stop.

Don's car was parked in front of Darryn's house when

she finally turned into his driveway and stopped in front of the gates. She checked the clock. It was three o'clock in the morning.

As she got out of the car, the front door opened and Don stepped out. She rushed forward, so glad to see a familiar face. He caught her in his arms.

"Hannah, I'm so glad you're here." He breathed while he held her close. "Are you—"

"I'm fine. Where's Darryn? How is he?" Her voice wobbled slightly on the last word.

"He'll live." Don smile was lopsided and he pulled her into the house. "He's sleeping at the moment."

"What did Stephen do to him?" She bit her trembling lip.

"Hit him with something—on his shoulder, his head. I have to warn you, he doesn't look good. His usually ugly face is even uglier." He chuckled and pressed a hand to her shoulder.

A sob escaped and Don took her arm. "Come and sit down, I've made tea." He handed her his phone. "But first, please call Caitlin."

He didn't have to say they were mad with worry at this point, she could just imagine.

"He threatened to hurt Darryn, to hurt my family," she tried to explain. "That's why I left. But now he's hurt him anyway," she ended on a near-sob.

"We thought that was probably what happened. What

you seem to forget is that we're family now. You're not alone in this. If you are in trouble, we all are; if you're unhappy, so are we. White succeeded in cutting you off from your family and friends—that's not a place where you have to be. You are not alone. Call your sister," he said again.

With unsteady fingers, she dialed Caitlin's number.

"Hannah?" It was her mom on the other side of the line.

Try as she might, she couldn't stop the tears. "Mom." She got the word out before the tears started falling.

"Sweetheart?" her mother asked in a broken voice. "Where are you? Are you okay?"

Hannah sniffed and wiped her face. "I'm okay, Mom. Mad as hell, but fine. I've just arrived at Darryn's house."

"Mad is good," her mother said, and she could hear the smile in her voice. "We're all mad now. You go to sleep now, you hear? We'll all be there tomorrow morning."

"Thanks, Mom," she said.

Smiling, Don took the phone from her while he pushed a cup of tea in front of her.

"Drink up. I've added something a little stronger to make you sleep."

"I want to…I need to see Darryn, please?"

"Of course. Drink up. I'll get your suitcase from the car."

A few minutes later she was standing next to Darryn's bed. Don had left the light on in the hallway. One side of Darryn's face was swollen. He was restless, turning his head, fidgeting with the sheets.

Swallowing her tears, she bent down and kissed his forehead.

"Hannah." He groaned without opening his eyes.

"I'm right here," she whispered and sat down next to him on the bed. She took his hand in hers, and he relaxed immediately.

When he was breathing calmly again, she tried to pull her hand out of his. She wanted to have a shower, put on clean clothes. But Darryn wouldn't let go of her hand. Lifting the sheets, she moved so she was lying next to him, his hand cradled in hers. There was time for a bath tomorrow, time to talk, to explain. But, right now, she just wanted to be close to him.

Chapter Twelve

HER SCENT FILLED his whole being, and Darryn woke up grunting. Damn, he knew it was a dream, but he could swear he felt her hand in his.

Something warm was nestled close to his side, and he looked down. His breath left his body in a whoosh. Lying next to him, on the side that hadn't been injured, one hand tucked under her chin, was Hannah. All her glorious hair was spread out over the pillow next to him.

A hole he didn't even know he had, filled up, over-flowed, and a peace he'd never experienced before settled over him. She was here, in his house, in his bed, she was fine, and he would make sure she stayed that way, even if it meant getting another blow to the head.

He tried to lift his hand; he wanted to touch her, but the pain in his shoulder left him gasping.

Her eyes flew open. "Hi." She smiled. "How are you feeling?" She lifted herself up on her elbow.

He stilled. If he lived to be a hundred, he would never forget this sight. Hannah, not quite awake yet, her hair all over the place, her blue eyes with traces of dreams still lurking in their depths, staring up at him, her mouth half-open. His heart stopped before it started beating erratically. He loved this woman with an intensity that left him aching for her.

"Damn, woman, you're a sight for sore eyes," he said gruffly and lifted the arm he could move. He touched her face, her hair, cupped her cheek. "You're really here. And you're not hurt."

"But you are." She gently slid her hands over the bandages on his head, her eyes filling.

"I'm fine," he said and caught her hand, bringing it to his lips. "Don't ever disappear like that again, you hear?" He growled and, catching her hair in his fist, he brought her mouth closer for a kiss.

Thirstily, he drank from her lips, reveled in her softness, her gentleness, and thanked his lucky stars she wanted to be here with him.

Out of breath, she finally lifted her head, trailing her fingers over his face, his jaw. "He warned me to stay away from you, otherwise he would hurt you and my family. That's why I had to leave, but then he hurt you anyway." She swallowed, her lip quivering.

He pulled her down for a quick kiss. "I underestimated him, not something that will happen again. The man is clearly deranged—no sane person would behave like this. According to my mother, he's been imitating me since school. I don't know what his problem is and frankly I don't care. We have arranged for a private detective, and Don called the police last night."

"The police?"

"Yeah, I know they're useless, but I think it's vital to lodge a formal complaint. They'll be here sometime this morning. You're not leaving my sight until that man is behind bars."

"She'll need strong coffee to put up with you then," Don said from the doorway and entered the room with a tray. "Three coffees coming up."

Darryn cleared his throat, touched his brother's hand briefly. "Thanks for staying."

"You're my baby brother," Don said gruffly before he held the tray out toward Hannah. "I'm actually sorry White didn't return—I was ready for him."

HANNAH'S THROAT CONSTRICTED as she watched the two brothers. Don put his hand lightly on Darryn's shoulder, the love and worry obvious in his touch.

The Cavallos might be hard businessmen, but from what she had witnessed thus far, they were also fierce protectors, as well as loyal and caring husbands, guarding what was theirs with great ardor.

She should have trusted Darryn and told him about Stephen's threat. If she'd done that, he wouldn't be lying here now, literally battered and bruised.

"Don't," he said, reading her mind. He pushed her hair back. "It's obvious now he would have come after me, no matter what you did or didn't do. None of this is your fault, please know that."

"I have a new phone for you." Don took the phone out of his pocket. "I had to get food—this guy's cupboards and fridge are totally empty, so I picked one up for you." He handed it to her. "Thought you'd need to get in touch with your agent."

"Thanks," Hannah said. "But Karen thought her phone may be bugged and…"

"The rest of the family will arrive soon and we can discuss this again, but my feeling is we have to flush out this guy. We know he's here, so Karen is, at least for the moment, safe. Call her. Also, I arranged for your hired car to be picked up. We'll drop you at your place later."

"Thanks." Hannah tried to get up from the bed, but Darryn pulled her down for another kiss.

"Don't go too far away, please?"

She smiled, touching his face. "Karen must be very worried. Let me phone her and then I'm going to take a shower."

Darryn's eyes darkened, and she remembered their previous conversation about showers.

"Take your call, but Don put your suitcase over there," Darryn said and pointed toward her bag sitting on a nearby chair. "Use my bathroom?"

She nodded and fled the room. Wow, he was hurt and his face swollen, but one look from his chocolate brown eyes had her nearly melting.

THE POLICE ARRIVED shortly after the rest of the family. Her sisters, Dana, her mother, and Darryn's mother, Rosa had pulled her in for a group hug.

"I'm so glad you're not hurt." Her mother sniffled and cupped Hannah's face. "You're my baby. I was going mad not knowing where you were."

"I'm so sorry," Hannah said, hugging her mom again. "But—"

Her mother patted her arm. "I know. There is a crazy person out there."

Darryn had refused to stay in bed. He was dressed, but still very pale. He pulled Hannah down next to him on the couch and took one of her hands in both of his.

Everyone sat down, and Don explained to the police what had been happening, including the attack on Darryn.

One of the two policemen looked at Hannah. "Let's leave last night's attack out of the picture for the moment. Can you give a detailed account of the incidents you think Stephen White has been involved in?"

"Not 'think.' We know!" Darryn interjected.

The policeman nodded, but kept his eyes on Hannah.

Her throat constricted. She didn't want to remember all

the horrible things that had happened over the last two years, let alone talk about them. But she also wanted this to stop.

Darryn tightened his hold on her hand, and she took a deep breath. With him by her side, she could do anything, even talk about Stephen bloody White.

Starting with Stephen getting fired because of her complaint, she listed the events that had happened chronologically.

"Do you have any concrete proof that everything that happened to you was this White fellow's doing?" the policeman asked.

"Well, I have…had the messages that he'd left on my phone, but I left that back in my apartment in Paris."

"I brought it with me." Caitlin rummaged through her bag. "I thought you might need it. I switched it off, and Don took the SIM card and battery out so it couldn't be traced." She handed the phone to the policeman.

"The trouble is, he never admitted to doing anything, although the only times I heard from him were after the incidents I've just told you about," Hannah said.

The two policemen looked at one another, then put the phone down on the coffee table.

One cleared his throat as he looked at Darryn. "And you think the person who attacked you last night was the same individual?"

Darryn glared at the policeman. "I don't think that, I know that. I was here, I saw, and I heard him. He said very clearly, 'She's mine.'"

The policeman coughed. "The doctor said you have a concussion. You don't think—"

"No, damn it, I don't 'think,'" Darryn said sarcastically. "I bloody well know it was him!"

The policemen got up. "If you could get us a report from your doctor?"

Darryn grunted. "Well, then, we'll—"

Caitlin's phone rang, and she stared at the device. "It's from the same number I received the message from last night—the one saying you were on your way," she said with a frown.

"It's my landlady on Jacobsbaai. Let me answer it," Hannah said and, with a feeling of apprehension, she stood up and took the phone.

"Hallo, it's Hannah," she said, trying to sound calm.

"Hannah, my dear, I…I don't even know why I'm telling you this, but the neighbors called me early this morning. The house…there was a fire, and the bedroom part of the house has been completely destroyed," she ended tearfully.

Hannah could feel all the blood leaving her face. The words penetrated her stunned brain. She understood what they meant, but she couldn't process the message. "A fire," she whispered. "In the bedroom where I would have been sleeping…"

Cursing, Darryn got up, but Don had already taken the phone from Hannah's limp fingers.

Hannah turned to Darryn. His face was even paler than before.

"What the hell happened?" He growled and pulled her close.

"There was a fire." She swallowed the bile that threatened to rise in her throat.

Her mother rushed forward, taking her hand. "Sweetheart." She couldn't get more out.

"The…house in Jacobsbaai, the bedroom where I slept…" Hannah inhaled quickly when she remembered. "I left the light on by accident, and only noticed it as I was driving away. I didn't want to waste time going back and switching it off, but I told the landlady about it." She stared at Don, who was still talking to the landlady. And the implication of what had happened finally sank in. "It's all my fault her beautiful home is ruined. Stephen figured out where I was, saw the light…" Hannah whispered, appalled by what had happened.

Darryn hugged her close. Everyone was now standing and staring at Don, who was still on the phone.

"Thank you for letting us know." Don ended the call.

"That means—"

"He knew where you were and thought you were still in the house," Caitlin barely got out. Her eyes were big. "He wanted to kill you," she whispered.

They all stared at Caitlin. Hannah tried to make sense of what she was hearing. Kill her? He had scared her, scared her sisters, and had hurt Darryn. And then he tried to kill her?

"What the hell more proof do you want?" Darryn growled, turning to the policemen. "There's a crazy man out there, and you need to find him!" he nearly shouted.

The policemen moved toward the front door. "We'll call the police stations in the neighboring towns of Saldanha and Vredenburg. Jacobsbaai doesn't have a police station. Let's see what we can find out."

Don got up and walked the policemen out. The rest of them stared at one another. David sat down and fiddled with his phone.

"Yeah, yeah, that's code for we don't believe you and you won't hear from us again," Darryn grumbled.

"What about that private detective?" Rosa asked Don. "Have you spoken to him? Does he have a plan?"

"We've spoken," he said, taking out his phone. "I'll find out what he knows."

"I've been searching on the Internet and there is an article on News24 about the fire," David said, scrolling down on his phone. "It clearly states that nobody was injured in the fire." He looked at Hannah. "So White will know you are still alive."

Hannah stared at David, her mind sluggishly processing what she was hearing.

"They didn't take your phone with them!" Zoe called out and picked up Hannah's phone that was still lying on the coffee table where the policeman had left it. "Let me see if they're still outside—"

"No, wait," Hannah said, finally coming out of her stupor. She put her hand out for the phone. Like yesterday morning, a calm settled over her. "He wants me, right? Well, let him find me." She closed her hand over the phone. "Where is the phone's battery?" she asked Caitlin.

"Are you completely crazy?" Darryn tried to take the phone from her.

But she moved away quickly and turned to face all of them. "You saw the policemen. They don't believe a word I'm saying. They will probably phone the police in Saldanha and wherever, but it's not going to happen today. And I'm done being scared, done running, done being the victim. This time I'm not alone, but Stephen doesn't know that. Let him find me," she repeated.

Darryn opened his mouth again, his hands fisted.

Dale put a hand on his shoulder. "She's right, you know? He's not going to stop before he does what he's set out to do. In his screwed-up mind, Hannah is the reason he lost his job and he—"

"'She's mine, I saw her first,'" Darryn murmured. "That's what he said before he hit me. So, in his mind, he saw you first and if he can't have you—"

"Nobody else will either. He'd rather me dead," Hannah said. "Well, let him try." Lifting her chin, she pushed her hair back.

Chapter Thirteen

DARRYN STARED AT Hannah, not sure whether he should hug her or throttle her. She lifted her chin.

Strong women. That was what David called his wife and his brothers' wives yesterday. And he loved a strong woman as well. Look at her. Her blue eyes were clear, her shoulders pushed back—she was ready to take on the world.

"I can't let you do that," he said in a soothing voice and stepped forward to pull her closer.

But she shook off his hand and turned her fiery blue eyes on him. "What did you say? *Let* me?" she asked, her voice ice cold.

"Oh, man, you shouldn't have said that." Dale snickered behind him.

"You never, ever tell them that." David guffawed.

"You have a lot to learn." Don, who had just finished his phone call, snorted.

"Oh, yeah?" Caitlin said coolly and turned to Don. "He's not the only one. Just the other day you tried to send us to the kitchen while we were looking for Hannah."

"I didn't send you to the kitchen, damn it to hell, I tried

120

to protect you!"

Caitlin crossed her arms and moved so she stood next to Hannah. Dana and Zoe joined them.

"So, now that you know we're quite capable of looking after ourselves," Caitlin said, "let us think of plan to get this bastard. All of us," she said. "Together."

Darryn swallowed all of his objections. He would find a way to keep Hannah safe, but that was clearly not something one said out loud. He was learning all right.

"I've spoken to the private detective," Don said. "He didn't know about the fire, but he followed White up to Langebaan before he lost him. I've told him White is probably on his way back."

"Well, hell," Darryn said. He wanted to storm outside, find the bastard, and kill him with his bare hands. But his head pounded, the roaring in his ears was back, and fatigue settled over him. He was bloody useless at the moment. Frustrated, he sat down.

Hannah dropped down next to him. "Won't you please lie down for a while? You're not going to be any help if you don't rest."

"Only if you come with me," he said, knowing full well he sounded like a petulant kid. But even if he couldn't do anything, he would feel better if Hannah was with him.

"Darryn, I'm not going to hide away here. I have a life, and I fully intend to carry on with it. I have a photo shoot tomorrow and have to find out more about it…"

"When did you hear about that? You only decided last night to come back?" Dana asked the question he was also wondering about.

"I spoke to Karen this morning. This came up a while ago when I didn't want to come to South Africa, but now that I'm here, I can do it. It's a shoot for an advertising campaign for one of the big retailers. There will be plenty of people around, so no need to worry about me."

She turned to Darryn. "You get your rest; I'll be back this evening."

He started to protest, but Zoe patted his shoulder. "Don't you worry, we won't leave her side."

"So what's the plan?" Zoe asked.

"I'm going to switch on my old phone again and keep it with me as well. If Stephen is so smart, he'll track me down. Only difference is, this time I'll be ready for him."

"You can't do this on your own," Darryn began hotly.

Hannah gave him a cool look. "I know. And I'm not going to. Fortunately, I have three big and bad brothers-in-law who can take turns following me around until you are better. And Don will also arrange for extra security."

"One that will not be duped and let you slip away?" Darryn asked.

Again her blue eyes rested on him coolly. "I told you, I'm sorry. You should know I won't do that again."

Darryn clenched his hands in frustration. He wanted to pick Hannah up, throw her over his shoulder, and take her to a place far away where no harm could come to her. But, damnit, he was so tired he could hardly stay awake, let alone protect anyone.

"May I talk to you for a second?" he asked and looked at Hannah.

She nodded and followed him to his room. "How are you feeling? Don't you think we should call—"

That was as far as she got because, kicking the door shut, he pulled her close to him and kissed her.

For a millisecond, she resisted, but he deepened the kiss, her mouth opened, and he gathered her close. He wanted a kiss. Just a kiss. But kissing Hannah Sutherland had never been "just" anything. Desire kicked him in the gut, sent his senses into overdrive, and with a groan he surrendered to her warmth, her softness.

Her kisses tied him up in knots and left him aching—not a physical ache that could be treated with bandages and ointments, but an ache for which the only cure was the woman in his arms. Why it took him two years to figure this out, he'd never know.

"I need to touch you," he said feverishly against her lips, and even before the words had left his mouth, he skimmed his hands over her breasts, cupped them, delighting in their softness. Her nipples hardened under his hands and, frantic to touch her flesh, he opened buttons, plucked aside satin and lace until his skin could touch hers.

He lifted his head, his breath coming out raggedly. With

her eyes glazed over, her heart pounding against his palm, he forgot about the people outside this room, life outside this house, danger somewhere in this city. The only thing that mattered was to become a part of Hannah as soon as humanly possible.

"I need you," he whispered and bent down to capture her lips with his again.

A loud pounding on his door had him cussing a blue streak.

"Hannah, we want to leave!" Don yelled, much louder than necessary.

"Yeah, we hear you!" Darryn growled back. "Just a damn minute."

He combed her hair back with his fingers.

"Tonight," he said. "I'll organize dinner." She had gathered the sides of her blouse, but he stopped her hands.

"Darryn, I have to go," she said.

"I know, but let me..." His hands cupped her breasts. Her breath hitched, and she licked her lips.

"Damn, woman." He growled and had to kiss her again. Reluctantly, he lifted his head, and with unsteady fingers, he helped her button up her blouse.

She smiled.

"Oh, you think it's funny driving me so nuts I can't hold my hands steady?" he said silkily and tugged her forward so she was in his arms again.

With one sweep of his hands, he moved the hem of her

short skirt all the way up over her hips so he could feel her heat. And watched as her eyes darkened.

"Darryn," she whispered and moved to give him better access.

"Hannah?" Caitlin's voice came from the other side of the door.

Hannah stepped back and finished buttoning her blouse. "Just a minute," she said.

"That's what Darryn said five minutes ago. You want me to come and pick you up later?" Caitlin asked, clearly amused.

"No, I'm on my way," she said before turning to him again.

"Don't switch your old phone back on before you get here tonight, please?" he asked. "I don't want that maniac to get close to you if I'm not around."

She stepped closer, lifted herself on her toes, and kissed his cheek. "See you tonight," she whispered, and before he could say anything, she was gone.

Darryn leaned against his bedroom door. His bothers were calling him to come out, but he needed a minute. His body had apparently forgotten he was suffering from a concussion. Feeling light-headed, he sat down on his bed as his door opened.

"You okay?" Dale asked.

"Yeah, I'm fine."

"Well, come and lock your front door, we don't want

that idiot returning and finding your door unlocked."

Grimacing, Darryn stood up. Well, that thought had the same effect as a bucket of ice-cold water. "Damnit, stop fussing." He growled but got up and followed a grinning Dale out of his room.

DARRYN WAS RESTLESS. After everyone had left this morning, he had slept for an hour and was now feeling much better. The doctor had been by, replaced the bandages and had advised him to stay home for another day or two before venturing outside.

He'd work on some photographs, but his thoughts kept straying to Hannah and damn Stephen White. Apparently Dale and a security guy were following her around today, but would they be able to keep her safe? There was an uneasiness in his gut he couldn't shake off.

Dale had phoned when he and the security guard left Hannah's home and followed her to the photo shoot. At his request, his brother had sent him the address where the shoot would take place. It was a venue in Sea Point he knew well and had worked in while he was still a fashion photographer.

Hannah was safe; she was being looked after by his brother and security guard. He should relax and try to finish the photographs he was working on.

Nothing could happen to her while she was doing the shoot, right?

So why the hell was he feeling this way? For a few seconds he stood still, trying to figure out what was wrong. Then he knew. His gut was trying to tell him something, and he had always relied on that.

Grabbing his car keys, he hurried to his car.

Chapter Fourteen

HANNAH SMILED AT the camera and moved to the instructions of the photographer, hoping she was pulling off looking relaxed and carefree. She was happier than she'd ever been before in her life; Darryn loved her, he wanted her, and the sparks flying around them whenever they came near one another were just about scorching. *But.* And because of that *but*, she had to make peace with the fact that people would be following her.

Apparently, Dale had lost today's bet, because he and a security guard dressed in civilian clothes had been following her around since she left her apartment late this morning. And although her brother-in-law was looking quite cheerful, she felt dreadful. They all had work to do; they had families of their own. It was ridiculous to have to traipse after their wives' sister because of some deranged idiot.

At this point she was so irritated, so mad about the whole thing, she wished Stephen White would show his face because she was ready for a fight.

Against Darryn's wishes, she'd put the battery back in her old phone, switched it on, and, although she was using her new phone, she kept the old one with her. If Stephen had been tracking her movements through her phone, she wanted him to find her. Darryn would probably be angry, but she was fed up with this cat-and-mouse game Stephen was playing. She mentioned it to Dale, and needless to say, he was also not very happy with what she'd done.

"Smile, sweetheart." The photographer coached her, and she realized she was scowling.

Trying to shut out everything around her, she moved and stretched and smiled until finally the photographer was happy.

The photographer walked over to her, smiling. "Thanks. It was a pleasure working with a professional like you," he said.

"I'm a bit distracted—sorry about the frown."

"Even frowning, you're gorgeous. Surely you know that?" He flirted, and she laughed.

This kind of light flirtation she could handle; most of the photographers did this with every model. Stephen White's creepy kind of flirting though, she couldn't stomach.

Smiling, she turned to go to the dressing room and that was when she felt it—the hairs on the back of her neck rising. He was here. Stephen White was somewhere close by. She continued walking and willed herself not to look around her.

She caught Dale's eye and with a quick motion of her head tried to warn him, but the frown on his forehead indicated he didn't understand what she was trying to say. He started forward, but a commotion behind her stopped everyone in their tracks, and all heads turned in that direction.

"Something is burning!" someone shouted. "Look, flames!"

Stephen White had a hand in this. She knew it.

Hannah glanced over her shoulder while she lengthened her strides. People were panicking, trying to get outside. She couldn't see Dale or the security guard through the smoke. She wanted to get to her phone as quickly as possible. At this point she could mostly see only smoke, but small flames were visible here and there against the opposite walls of the building. Around her, people were shouting and running toward the front door.

Hannah rushed forward, but a strong hand grabbed her shoulder and something poked her in her back.

"If you hadn't flirted with the photographer, I wouldn't have had to start a fire." A voice hissed in her ear.

A chill went down her spine. Stephen White. "Now put your hair up under this hoodie, walk toward the door, and don't try and draw anyone's attention, especially not the attention of Cavallo and what I assume is a security guard." He snickered. "Don't you know by now nobody can keep me away from you? Now walk, I have a gun at your back."

Hannah did as she was told. A strange calmness settled over her. This was going to end today, one way or another.

This man was not going to hurt anyone else, not if she could help it. There was no way she was getting into a car with him and she had a plan, but for it to work, she didn't want anyone else too close to them, so leaving the building was a good idea.

DARRYN PHONED DALE when he reached Sea Point, about a block away from the building. He'd made the journey in record time. Fortunately, it wasn't peak time for the traffic yet and he could drive relatively fast. But he had to know whether Hannah was still okay.

Dale's phone only rang and rang and, swearing, Darryn dialed the number again. This time his brother answered.

Before Dale answered, sounds of people running and shouting interrupted. An icy-cold hand closed around his heart.

"What happened?" he barked.

"Hannah…she's gone," Dale said. "I think White took her. I've phoned Don, and he'll contact the police. Someone started a fire. It's small and they have been able to contain it, but—"

"I'm close," Darryn shouted before Dale had finished talking. He threw down his phone and stepped on the gas. The roaring in his ears made it impossible to think, to talk. His instincts kicked in, and the only thought in his mind was getting to Hannah. He had to protect her. Life without her wasn't worth living. It was that simple. And if Stephen White did something to her, hurt her in any way, he would pay.

As he neared the building, he saw smoke billowing out of the windows on one side. The sound of sirens rang out. Good. Fire engines were heading toward them. People hurried outside through the big front doors.

With screeching brakes, he stopped his car and jumped out while he scanned the faces of the people passing him. He would recognize Hannah's hair anywhere.

Frantically, he moved forward. He couldn't see her. Think, Cavallo, think! What would that bastard do? He would try to get her outside as soon as possible.

As he turned around, Dale and the security guard came running out. Damn it, White probably knew that Hannah had people watching over her.

"Do you see her anywhere?" Dale asked.

"How long since the shoot?" Darryn asked, ignoring Dale's stupid question. If he'd seen her, he wouldn't be standing there, damn it!

"It probably only five minutes ago, although so much else has happened since."

"Then they must still be close by," Darryn said while he scanned the crowd. He noticed the parking area behind the building and pointed toward it.

"Let's have a look over there," he said. "He probably parked his car where he would be able to take off quickly—

let's check the area." He began jogging, ignoring the head-ache behind his eyes.

STEPHEN PUSHED THE gun against her back. "The black van over there." He shoved her forward.

Hannah gnashed her teeth. Her high heels weren't meant to be worn during long walks and definitely not when she was being pushed around, but she didn't want to take them off just yet. They were going to come in handy quite soon.

She was mad as hell. This idiot had messed up her bud-ding relationship with Darryn two years ago, he'd hurt her, he had hurt her sister, and had hurt Darryn. Her mind raced. She didn't have much time left, and if she wanted to get away, she had to do it very soon.

"So where are all the Cavallos now?" His laugh was high, near hysterical. Stephen yanked her against his body with his one arm. "You're all alone. Not even Darryn Cavallo is in sight!"

The guy probably hadn't had a shower in days, and he also had too much to drink; the stench wafting from him was overwhelming. She swallowed against the nausea that rose in her throat, but she kept still.

"No, it's only you and me, Stephen. Isn't that what you've always wanted?" she said sweetly.

His arm stilled around her body. "That's right," he said. "You and me, I like the sound of that." And again his high-pitched laughter followed.

They reached the car. She would have one chance. That was it.

Stephen's one arm dropped from her body as he fiddled in his pocket, probably looking for his car keys.

"I—"

"Stand still!" he ordered, yanking her back again. He unlocked the passenger door of the car.

"I only want to take my shoes off, they're hurting me. Surely you won't mind that?" Hannah asked meekly and moved so she leaned against the car.

Stephen came closer, still wielding the gun.

She bent forward and took off one shoe. "Put away the gun. I'm here, and I'm not going anywhere," she said, not looking at him.

Slowly, she bent down to take off the other shoe while looking at Stephen from the corner of her eye. He played with the gun for a few seconds, but then put it in his pocket.

"Just don't try anything," he said and turned slightly to scan the area.

This would be her only chance. Hannah grabbed her shoe and clutched it tightly in both her hands. Stephen moved his feet so his back was turned in her direction. This was it. With all the built-up anger inside of her, she brought down the sharp heel, aiming it straight at the back of his head.

DARRYN JOGGED AROUND the building and froze.

About few feet in front of him was White and a woman. It took his stunned brain a few seconds to realize it was Hannah. She was wearing a hoodie and was still dressed in a short, tight dress she had probably been wearing for the shoot.

But what turned his blood to ice was what she was doing. Her gaze was on White's back, and she was clutching something in her hands. As he watched, she lifted her arms. She wanted to clobber him with it!

"Is that Hannah?" Dale's incredulous voice came from behind him.

His feet were moving before he knew what he was doing. He had to get to Hannah, had to help her. He raced forward, bellowing her name. White turned around to face him at the same moment Hannah's arms moved and she brought whatever she was holding down on White's head.

For a split second, White stared at him, a stupefied expression on his face before he swore and grabbed his head. He staggered away.

Stunned, Darryn stared at Hannah. Her eyes were bright, her chin held high. She was gloriously, magnificently, beautifully angry.

"What a woman," he murmured, gave one more stride, and then Hannah was in his arms.

"Hannah." He breathed, holding her shaking body tightly against him and losing his heart, his body, his soul, his very being all over again.

Behind him, his two other brothers, who had apparently also just arrived, were talking excitedly. To his right, policemen were grabbing White, but Darryn didn't turn around, didn't move an inch.

He had his whole world in his arms, and he didn't know whether he would ever be able to let her go.

Chapter Fifteen

"WELL, FROM NOW on, I'll have more respect for these killer heels," Don teased, picking up the shoe Hannah had brought down on White's head.

Hannah inhaled sharply. "I didn't kill him."

"I know." Don smiled and patted her back. "I'm just teasing. You're part of a clan of strong women," he said, putting his arm around his wife.

David pulled Dana closer. "I'm proud to say I'm also married to one of those, even if she isn't a Sutherland. You should have seen my wife when her life was in danger."

"Yeah, yeah, you've told that story so many times we all know about the flower pot she was going to use to clobber him with," Dale teased.

"Is the guy who tried to attack her still in jail?" Don asked.

Darryn pulled Hannah close to him, tuning out the rest of the voices. After White had been taken into custody, he'd brought Hannah back to his house. Everyone else followed them here, and the story had to be told over and over again. And as much as he loved his family, he would have loved it even more if they all left right now. He wanted, no, he *needed* to be alone with Hannah.

"So it's really over?" Hannah's mother asked and sat down next to them on the couch.

"It's really over." Hannah smiled and leaned forward to hug her mom. "Stephen is in custody; there will probably be a trial at some point, but I'm not going to think about that now."

Her mother clutched her hand even tighter. "He obviously went completely off the rails at the end. I'm just so happy nothing happened to you. Are you sure you're okay? Don't you think you should talk to someone about this whole thing?"

Hannah shook her head. "I'm trying not to dwell on what happened, but rather be thankful I'm here and I'm safe. And, you're right, I don't think Stephen was thinking rationally toward the end. According to the police, he's had psychiatric problems since his teens, that whole thing of wanting to be like Darryn, for instance. The fact that I got him fired fueled whatever anger he has been carrying inside him all along. I was the final 'thing' he didn't want Darryn to have."

"I suppose one should feel sorry for him, but he wanted to hurt my little girl," her mother said, hugging her close.

"I'm fine now, Mom. I know you can't wait to go back to your writing again, so don't worry about me. I really am all right. When are you starting a new story?" Hannah asked, hoping to get her mother's attention focused on something else.

Her mother's eyes twinkled as she got up. "Well, I'll have to adjust my usual love story to include a villain this time, it seems."

"Mom, please don't tell me you are going to be writing about this?" Hannah asked exasperated.

"Who, me?" her mother asked with a poker face. "I wouldn't dream of it," she said and bent down to kiss Hannah on the cheek.

"She is so going to write about this," Hannah grumbled. "She's written stories about all her other daughters' and Dana's love lives. You would think she has enough material without adding me to the lot."

"It's high time you get a turn," Caitlin said.

"But Hannah's story isn't finished yet," her mother said serenely.

Hannah jumped up. "I've had enough excitement to last me a lifetime, Mom—this is my story, the end!" She hugged her mother. It was impossible to stay irritated with her mother for long. "Are you leaving with Caitlin and Don?"

"No, my car is outside." She touched Hannah's face. "Now that I know you're not in danger any more, I'll gladly go back to Hermanus."

"Let me walk you out," Hannah said.

"Wait, we're all leaving," Caitlin said with a wink in Darryn's direction. "I can feel when I'm not wanted."

Darryn grinned. "I'm not going to apologize for wanting to be alone with Hannah."

"So, you're finally admitting you've had a thing for Hannah all along?" David asked and slapped him on the back. "And that despite everything you said to the contrary."

Darryn got up. "Well, it took me a while." Grinning, he looked at his brothers. "Like it took all of you a while to figure out you want these women in your lives," he said and waved his hand in the direction of his sisters-in-law.

His mother stepped closer and cupped his face. "You still have a long way to go," she smiled.

"What do you mean?" he asked, but Hannah was clearing her throat, and everybody turned to look at her.

Darryn looked at her, and his heart dipped. What he felt for Hannah was so much more than a "thing" as his brothers so eloquently put it. He was crazy about her.

"I...I don't know how to thank all of you for what you've done. You've put your lives on hold, flown across continents, disrupted your daily routines—and all to help watch over me. I won't ever forget it," she ended in a whisper.

"Group hug!" Caitlin shouted in a wobbly voice, and everyone huddled together for a hug.

Darryn moved so he was behind Hannah. As he put his arms around her body, she folded her hands around his. She fit beautifully in his arms.

"Okay, enough crying for one day." Hannah's mom sniffled and everyone stepped back. "I want to be back home before dark."

HANNAH CLOSED HER mother's car door. "Drive safely and let us know when you're home," she said and bent down to kiss her mom.

Her mom touched her face and beamed. "I'm so glad you and Darryn have finally sorted out your differences. You two belong together; it's so obvious. So, what happens now?"

Hannah stepped back from the car. "We're together, Mom, nothing else is going to happen. My schedule is full. I'll probably be around for another day or two before I have to fly to New York. I don't know whether I've told you, but I'll be part of the Victoria's Secret Fashion Show again this year."

"That's wonderful, my dear!" her mom gushed. "This will be what? The third time you're one of the angels?"

Hannah nodded. "Yes, it is. I'm looking forward to it. It's always so much fun."

Her mother cocked her head. "How do you really feel about going away, being so busy, being away from Darryn? And what does he say?"

"Drive safely, Mom." Hannah smiled and waved.

Her mom laughed. "You don't have to answer me, but do think about the questions, my dear." She reversed the car out of the driveway.

Hannah waved and watched her mom's car until it disappeared around the corner. Behind her, the rest of their family were also getting into cars while talking and laughing. Things were finally back to normal.

She would have to talk to Darryn about her schedule. Her life had always been so busy, and she never had anyone else to consider besides herself. But at this point, she wasn't sure what she and Darryn were.

She turned around and looked at Darryn. He was talking to his dad and laughed at something he'd said. Her heart did its usual silly little dance when he was around and she sighed.

Damn, she loved this man, always had and always would. Even if he only wanted her for a little while, that was also fine; she had no pride left when it came to Darryn Cavallo. She wanted him something fierce, and if a few days, a few months were all they'd have, then she'd be happy. At this point, she would take what she could get.

Last goodbyes were called out and finally the last car drove away.

Darryn turned to her with a smile.

"I love my family, but damn, I'm glad they're all gone now." He put his arm around her as they moved toward the front door.

"How are you feeling?" Hannah asked as he closed the door behind them. "Headache better?"

"I'm fine," he said with a light in his eyes that left her dry-mouthed. "Why do you ask?"

Her hands moved without any direction from her brain and lifted her top over her head. Her own brazenness startled her, but her body knew no shame. She wanted Darryn, and after all the fear and worry of the past two years, she was done overthinking this. She wanted him and she had been waiting long enough.

"I wanted to make sure you can handle this," she teased as she unzipped her jeans and shimmied out of them. She took a deep breath. All she was wearing was a blue G-string and a matching lace bra.

Darryn stepped closer, his eyes molten chocolate. He had his hands in his pockets, and the only movement was the flaring of his nostrils. His whole body was tense, the muscles on his arms flexed. The temperature in the room increased rapidly, but he didn't touch her.

His heated gaze traveled slowly over her, scorching her skin as his gaze moved downward.

Immediately, her body reacted to his bold stare. And he hadn't even touched her yet.

His gaze lingered on her breasts, and her nipples hardened. When he looked up again, his eyes were black with desire.

He exhaled slowly. "You are so beautiful, I can't believe you're here, with me, like this."

She moved forward, stepped boldly between his legs. "Believe it," she whispered and unbuckled his belt.

He dropped his forehead against hers. "I'm scared to take

my hands out of my pockets, scared that I might hurt you. I've wanted you so desperately for so long, I…"

But she had stopped listening. She unzipped his pants, pushed them down. He faltered, and she slowly began unbuttoning his shirt, concentrating on her task.

With each movement of her hands, another part of his rock-hard muscles was revealed, a part she had no choice but to touch, to caress, to kiss until he was shuddering under her hands.

Against her tummy, his desire was growing, making her light-headed. By the time she finally unbuttoned the last button, pushed away the sides of his shirt, and spread her hands over his muscled, gorgeous body, she was shivering with need.

Her fingers trailed over his shoulder where Stephen had hit him. It was black and blue and had to be so sore. But before she could ask, he picked her up and caught her lips with his. He tripped over his pants, cussed against her lips before he deepened the kiss, and pinned her against the wall.

SHE WAS KILLING him. Desperate to touch as much of her as quickly as possible, Darryn's hands streaked down her sides. She was rose petals and satin, velvet and heat. He could spend days touching her skin, investigating every smooth line, every soft curve of her gorgeous body, but she had unleashed something inside of him and, although he was trying to hold on to his sanity, he was losing his grip fast.

With deft movements, he got rid of the last pieces of clothing. Lifting his head, he cupped her breasts, watching in wonder how perfectly they fit in his hands. He bent down, caught one nipple in his mouth, and lost a little bit of his reason as her scent surrounded him. The whole of the outside world ceased to exist. All that mattered was loving this woman, showing her exactly how much he wanted her.

"Darryn," she whispered, her head moving restlessly against the wall.

"Yeah?" he asked, making sure her other breast got the same treatment.

"I...I need you. Now," she demanded, her hands moving restlessly over him.

Claiming her mouth again, his hands moved down so he could cup her. She was ready for him. The need to be one with her roared through his blood, and with her name on his lips, he lifted her higher against the wall and pushed into her.

Sobbing, she folded her legs around his body.

"Look at me?" he asked through clenched teeth while trying to focus on her face.

Her blue eyes were dark with passion, her lips swollen with his kisses. Without taking his eyes off of her, he began to move. She bit her lip and trembled against him and he lost the last vestiges of his control.

HANNAH TRIED TO keep her gaze on Darryn.

Passion had darkened his eyes. His teeth were clamped together as he began to move inside her. Her body instinctively followed his rhythm, she tried to concentrate on every single detail. She wanted to remember this moment forever.

But Darryn threw back his head, gathered her close to him, and she let the gale force of sensation pick her up and fling her far away.

When she next opened her eyes, they were lying entangled on the floor. She had landed on top of him, his arms protectively folded around her.

"Wow." Hannah breathed without lifting her head. "Yep—you are definitely fine." She moved her head so she could look at Darryn.

His eyes were still closed, a smile hovered around his mouth, and he looked more relaxed than she'd seen him in a long time. His hand was trailing up and down her back, igniting the flames that were still simmering just below the surface. She bent down, intending to simply press her lips against his hurt shoulder, but his warm skin invited her to linger.

Under her hand, the beating of his heart stopped for a second before it picked up the pace. Smiling, she slid lower down his body, her lips trailing kisses over his torso, down over his muscled tummy until his skin quivered beneath her lips.

"Hannah," he said through clenched teeth and tried to

grab her arms.

But she moved down his body all the way, shaking her head. "My turn to love you," she said and bent her head.

DARRYN BARKED OUT a short laugh and tried to grab her shoulders again so he could stop her. There was no way in hell he was going to last and he wanted to be inside her. But she lowered her head, and he forgot what he wanted to do, forgot what he wanted to say, and fell back on the floor.

Passion was a red haze that was blurring his vision, and he tried to fight it back, but it was too overwhelming, too devastating—he couldn't do anything else but ride the wave until he crested triumphantly, shouting out her name.

Chapter Sixteen

L IFE INTRUDED EARLY the next morning while they were having breakfast. His phone rang.

Darryn got up from the table and motioned toward his phone. "It's Don. I'd better take it."

"Of course." Hannah got up and started clearing away their dishes.

"You don't have to do that," he said, his gaze stuck on her long, bare legs. She was wearing one of his old T-shirts and looked much better in it than he ever had.

"I know, but I want to." She smiled, and he turned away to answer his phone.

"Yes?" he barked. He wasn't really interested in what his brother had to say.

"Sorry to intrude, but we have hotels to run," Don said, clearly amused. "How are you feeling?"

"I'm fine, and I know we're running hotels. I'll be in later—"

"Make that earlier rather than later; we can't postpone this meeting again," Don said.

Darryn sighed and moved his shoulder slightly. It was

still sore, but at least he was able to move it now. He'd known since yesterday that life would have to return to normal at some point, but he'd hoped for a couple more days alone with Hannah.

"Right, see you later," he said.

"Are you sure you're feeling up to going into the office?" Hannah asked.

He walked over to her and put his arms around her. "What do you think?" he asked, kissing her neck.

She turned in his arms with a smile. Damn, she was beautiful. She literally took away his breath each time she was this close.

"I know," she said and gave him a hug. "You have to go, and I have to fly to New York early tomorrow morning, but—"

Stunned, Darryn stared at her. "What?"

She cocked her head. "You know what I do, right? You know the schedule, more or less. It hasn't changed. I travel. I'm seldom here. This is what I do."

Thousands of different thoughts raced through his head. Damnit, he wasn't ready to let her go yet.

He hadn't figured out exactly how this would work. "But...but we are...together now, aren't we?" he asked, realizing he didn't quite know how to define their relationship.

She smiled and folded her arms around his neck. "I love you, and yes we are together, if that's what you want to call it, but you have work, I have work." She kissed him softly. "We'll figure it out as we go along; don't fret about it."

He kissed her forehead. "I love you too," he said slowly. "But I don't know how to let you go. I've been angry with you for two years, I've worried about you for two years, I've loved you for two years, and now we're finally..." He motioned with his hand between them, still not sure what to call what they had.

"Together?"

He kissed her hard. "We're much more than that and you know it." He looked at his watch. "What time is your flight?"

"Early, but don't worry. I'll take a taxi—"

"What time?"

"Quarter to six."

He winced and she giggled. "Told you! Really, Darryn, I've been doing this for—"

He kissed her. "You'll be sleeping here. I'll take you," he said between kisses. Damn, he couldn't get enough of her.

"Didn't you say you had to go to the office?" Hannah asked.

He lifted her up on the kitchen counter. "Yeah, I'll be late," he whispered, moving his hands up her legs so he could spread them.

"I'm not wearing..."

His hands stilled because he'd discovered it himself. "Panties." He gasped, as need heated his blood in milliseconds. "Damn, woman, you'll be the death of me yet," he groaned and lowered his head.

DARRYN HAD A firm grip on her elbow as they walked toward the airport building. Hannah felt like crying and she knew exactly why. She didn't want to go. She didn't want to leave Darryn. But it was ridiculous to feel like this. She loved her job. She loved the traveling. Just because she had a boyfriend now didn't mean she should stop living her life.

"You really could have dropped me off. Now *you're* wasting time."

He swung her around so that they faced one another. "No time spent with you is wasted. This way, I get to be with you for a little bit longer." He sounded angry.

"Darryn, you can't be angry every time I leave."

He started walking again, his arm around her. "I know."

She glanced at him, but his face was closed, his eyes hidden behind sunglasses. He stood next to her while she checked in her luggage and kept his arm around her until she had to go through to the departure hall.

At the security gates, he pulled her to the side so the passengers behind them could pass.

"Enjoy," he said and brushed her hair over her shoulder.

"I'll miss you," she said and tried a smile while swallowing desperately against the lump in her throat. If she started crying now, she wasn't going to stop.

Darryn pulled her close for a kiss. His lips lingered, his breathing became ragged, and just when she was on the brink of forgetting where they were, he dropped his hands.

"So, I'll see you?"

Hannah touched his face. "In about three weeks. I should be able to come back before the Paris fall and winter show. But then I'm not sure. There are various shoots, and in September there is…"

"Fashion week in almost every country, I remember," Darryn said and kissed her forehead. "Call me when you land?" he asked. "And please stay safe?"

She nodded, incapable of speech. With a last wave, she turned her back on him and proceeded through the security check.

Once she had her bag and laptop back in her hands, she looked over her shoulder. Darryn was still standing in the same spot, hands in his pockets, staring at her.

Her heart just about jumped out her breast and she sighed. Pasting on another smile, she waved cheerily before she turned back to follow the other passengers. Her heart was breaking—everything inside her was urging her to turn back, to forget about New York, to forget about her appointments, and to go and be with Darryn.

She sniffled. Damn it, she was being silly, of course she couldn't just drop everything because she now had a boyfriend! They were together—whatever that meant. How long this togetherness lasted was anybody's guess; she had never done this before.

Her phone rang as she sat down to wait for her boarding time. Her heart did a silly dance, but it was her mom, not Darryn, who called.

"At the airport?" her mom asked after she answered.

"Yes, Darryn just dropped me off."

"Oh, isn't that sweet of him!" Her mother gushed. "Now that's the kind of thing the hero in my story will do!"

Hannah sighed. "This is real life, Mom, not a story."

"It's your story, my dear child. And don't you forget it. It's the decisions you make that write your story."

Hannah was silent for a moment, blinking back silly tears. "I'm not the only one involved in my story, Mom," she said softly.

"But Darryn loves you, didn't he tell you that?"

"Yes, he does now, but what about next week or next month or…"

"Oh, my sweet child, the man is head over heels with you. He has been for two years. Why would it change now?"

"Because now I've told him I love him. He may decide I'm not who he thought I was after all. Remember, although I've known him for two years, we haven't spent much time together."

"Do you think your feelings for him will change?" her mother asked.

"Of course not, but—"

"So why assume his will?"

Hannah rolled her eyes. There was no talking to her romance-besotted mother. "Oh, Mom, you of all people know what men are like. My own dad didn't even stick around. Besides, Darryn is a Cavallo. He could have any woman he wants."

Her mother sighed. "I'll tell you what I've told your sisters as well. Yes, your dad left us when you were little. But his leaving wasn't anyone's fault but his own. And sweetheart, not all men leave. From what I've seen, the Cavallos are fiercely loyal and loving husbands."

"Well, that's another thing. Three of them are married to two of my sisters—I've never heard of anything so...so bizarre! Brothers involved with sisters, what are the odds?"

Her mother laughed out loud. "Love happens, Hannah, in strange and delightful ways. It's not something you can order according to certain rules. If it happens, it happens and, sweetheart, it's a rare thing for two souls to meet. Don't turn your back on your chance, promise me?"

Around her, people were walking toward the exit.

Hannah sighed. "I promise. Mom, I have to board. I'll let you know when I land in New York."

"Think about what I've said!"

Hannah put her phone away and fell into the queue. When she had seen Darryn for the first time, love happened. She didn't decide, she didn't choose, it simply...happened.

Clutching her bag, she walked toward the big plane that would carry her over an ocean, over a continent—far away from Darryn.

Another tear threatened to spill over, and she sniffled angrily. Damn it, she had work to do. Work that she loved. This was her life!

Besides, modeling helped her to achieve her big dream to help children who couldn't help themselves. Being able to help start a fund for war orphans had been something she had wanted to do for a long time, and through her modeling she now had the money and the connections to make life a little bit easier for the kids left in the wake of the devastation of war.

Squaring her shoulders, she lengthened her stride. She'd be back in three weeks. Maybe Darryn would be waiting for her at the airport, maybe he wouldn't. But she was not going to hold her breath.

Somewhere over the Atlantic, she opened her tablet. Caitlin, Zoe, and Dana had made boards on Pinterest after they got married. Why she wanted to torture herself to look at these now, she had no idea. But a few minutes later, she had created her own board and was looking through all things wedding-related without understanding why.

Chapter Seventeen

"AND WHO ATE your porridge this morning?" Don asked and slapped him on the back.

Darryn scowled, trying to concentrate on the computer. "I'm working."

He shared an open plan office with his brothers. They each had smaller offices they used when they needed more privacy, but they all preferred this open space. Usually, it worked very well, because it made discussing their work easy. But maybe he should have worked in his own office for another day or two.

He had been avoiding joining them here over the last two weeks since Hannah's departure. Damnit, his brothers were all ecstatically happy, and he was miserable, even more miserable than he'd been before he told Hannah he loved her.

Since Hannah's departure, they'd talked over the phone, they'd Skyped, they'd texted, they'd emailed one another, but it wasn't the same as being with her, being able to touch her, to smell her, to love her. He slept alone, he got up in an empty bed and empty house, he had his meals alone, and he hated every minute he was not with her.

And to add to his frustration, he found he kind of clammed up when he was talking to her over the phone or via Skype. He had never been good with words. Showing her how he felt about her wasn't a problem. The problem was she wasn't near him, so he couldn't demonstrate what he felt. And the longer she stayed away, the worse it became. He didn't want to talk to her about his day, his work. He wanted…her.

He was being irrational, but damnit, ever since he first laid eyes on Hannah Sutherland, his brain had stopped working rationally.

He somehow thought if he was among his brothers, he might not miss her so much. It wasn't working, and to add to his frustration, he had to sit there and listen to his brothers' smart remarks.

"How are you feeling?" Dale asked. "Head and shoulder working again?"

"I'm fine." Darryn growled and continued looking at his computer.

"He doesn't sound fine to me," David said. "What do you guys think?"

"It's not as if he's been Mr. Sunshine over the last two years, but lately he's downright grumpy," Dale complained.

Irritated, Darryn looked up. "I'm right here, you know? You want to say something to me, say it."

"I don't know why you're so grouchy. I thought you got

the girl," David said innocently.

"Yes, damnit, I got the girl, but she...she's in New York. She's working," he snapped and again tried to concentrate on what he was supposed to be doing.

"Women work," Dale said. "Zoe still works as an interior designer. She flies to London in two weeks."

"And you don't mind?" Darryn asked.

"We discuss our schedules and, whenever possible, I go with her." A grin nearly split his face in two. "Just so happens I can go with her this time."

"Caitlin still sees patients," Don said. "Of course it helps that she now has her rooms adjacent to the house. With Donato getting bigger, it's more difficult, but we try to work our schedules out so one of us is always with him. It's not always possible of course, but we have the loving grandmas on standby."

"And Dana still teaches. I actually thought she would stop working once we were married, but she loves what she does."

"But they don't work halfway across the world all the time," Darryn said. "She'll be back in a week's time, but then she's off again somewhere and then she'll be away for months!"

"Oh, man you've got it bad." David grinned. "Have you told her you loved her?" Dale asked.

"Of course, I damn well told her!" Darryn exclaimed. "What a bloody stupid question!" A blessed silence fell over the office.

Darryn tried to concentrate on his work.

"You could go with her when she has to be away," Dale said.

"Yeah, what you do, you can do anywhere and, frankly, if you're going to be this grumpy every time she leaves, you may just as well go with her," David said.

"And..." Don began, but Darryn had had enough. Swearing, he got up and grabbed his computer.

"I'll be working in my office," he snarled and stormed out.

"ENJOYING NEW YORK?" Caitlin asked, and Hannah smiled as she closed her apartment door behind her.

Balancing the cell phone between her chin and her shoulder, she kicked off her shoes, threw down her bag, and flopped down on the couch. "It's spring over here, so yes, New York is lovely."

"And the rehearsals for the show?"

"It's fun. I'm enjoying it."

"But?" Caitlin asked.

"But nothing," Hannah said, trying to sound cheerful. "We've been so busy, and the days are crazy, I..."

"Miss Darryn?" Caitlin interjected, clearly amused.

Hannah sighed. It was no use, Caitlin knew her too well. "Yes, I do. Something crazy. I've been in love with him for two years, during which time I hardly saw him but now, after we've been together, I can't sleep, I can't eat, damn it, I can't stop thinking about him! This is crazy!"

"Surely you talk over the phone or Skype?"

"Yes, of course we do, but with the time difference and our schedules, it's not always possible."

"But you're back in a week?"

"Yes, but I have to leave again after a month. I have to be in Europe from middle of June probably until October. And then I'll have to go to New York for the Victoria's Secret's show, which means I'll only be back, oh hell, I don't know when!" Hannah nearly wailed.

"Sounds to me like you have decisions to make," Caitlin said softly.

"What do you mean?"

"I mean you're obviously not happy being so far away from Darryn, and there is a very simple solution."

"Oh, yeah? And what is that?"

"Marry Darryn, stay with him. Help manage the children's foundation you're involved with from Cape Town, and do the odd modeling gig whenever you feel like it."

Hannah didn't know whether to laugh or cry. "Simple? There is nothing simple in your suggestion! First of all, I've worked very hard to be where I am today; I don't know whether I want to simply drop everything for a man."

"So when will you want to stop, do you think?" Caitlin asked.

"I don't know, there never has been a reason to think about quitting. In a few years, probably, when I'm ready."

"So the fact that you're now in a relationship doesn't change how you feel about being away so much?"

"Am I? In a relationship, that is? Which brings me to my second point: I can't marry a guy who hasn't asked me to marry him! Yes, he told me he loves me, but he hasn't said it once since I've been in New York. We could be brother and sister the way he talks to me. It doesn't sound as if we're in a 'relationship.' Maybe he's found someone else, maybe—"

"Hannah, stop!" Caitlin exclaimed. "Listen to yourself!" She sighed. "You're a gorgeous woman. Any man would be lucky to be near you, and Darryn has been in love with you ever since I met him. You've been through this horrendous ordeal with a madman, and when Darryn finally knew what was going on, he left without a suitcase to be with you. And, Hannah, once the Cavallos fall in love with someone, that's it for them. Look at all of them!"

"The obvious difference is they all wanted to get married. Darryn hasn't said a word again about love, never mind about getting married. And it's fine. I'd rather know now that he's not going to stick around, than find out later like Mom did."

Caitlin sighed audibly over the phone. "Oh, Hannah. You were younger than me and Zoe when Dad left. I didn't think his leaving would also leave a scar on you. Dad is...Dad." She laughed. "I don't think I ever told you, but when I realized how I felt about Don, I wanted to see Dad. I wasn't sure why. We met at the Waterfront, and while we were talking, he was shamelessly ogling a woman at a nearby table. And then I realized—Don is so different. He has eyes only for me, like David has for Dana, and Dale for Zoe. Not all men are like Dad, thank goodness. Watch the brothers and their dad. Their eyes are stuck on their loved one—it's a wonderful thing to see."

"You sound like Mom," Hannah said glumly.

"Darryn loves you, we can all see that."

"But he hasn't said anything again!"

Caitlin giggled. "Well, sweetie, it so happens that you have a mother who writes romance novels. I'm sure you can steal some of her ideas to make the telephone conversations …how shall I put it? More interesting? Come to think of it, Mom's stories may be too tame for what you need; I'll send you a link for a book I heard about. And remember, the poor man doesn't always have to be the first to say or do anything. We are twenty-first century women. I mean, look at you—you didn't even wait for your knight in shining armor to rescue you from the dragon's clutches—you clobbered the dragon with your high heel!"

A giggle escaped Hannah's lips, and soon she and Caitlin were laughing uncontrollably.

"Thank you, I needed a good laugh," Hannah said after the giggles finally stopped.

"Call him. I'm sure he'd love to hear from you," Caitlin

ordered before they ended the call.

By FIVE O'CLOCK the next morning, Hannah was still wide awake, staring at her ceiling. She couldn't sleep. She'd cleaned her apartment, made sure her schedule was up to date, sent out emails, and scrolled through the books on her tablet, struggling to find something that would interest her. And although she'd began reading one or two of the books, her mind was too busy to focus on the words in front of her, and she'd switched off the light at midnight, hoping to fall asleep.

But thoughts of Darryn kept her awake. No, make that *longing* for him kept her awake. She missed him. Badly. And Caitlin's words also kept turning in her head. Marry Darryn. Stay with him.

Could she do that? Could she give up everything she'd worked so hard for? Her career was at a point where she was able to choose the jobs she wanted to do. If Darryn insisted she stop working, would she do that? Did she want to do that?

Her phone beeped. She sat up, switched on her bedside lamp, and looked at her phone. It was a message from Caitlin with a link. Frowning, she opened the link.

The link opened on a site where a book was advertised. On the cover of the book was the muscled chest of a very sexy cowboy. Giggling, she remembered Caitlin did say something about sending her a book she'd heard about.

She bent down to pick up her tablet where she'd dropped it the previous night and, sitting back against the pillows, opened the e-reader, clicked on the muscled torso, and started reading.

A few pages into the book, she grabbed an envelope that was lying on the side table and began to fan herself. Oh, my goodness—did people do this?

And the more difficult question: could *she* do this? Did she have the guts to pull this off? Out of breath, she put down the tablet, several interesting thoughts racing through her head.

She'd never thought of herself as brazen, but when she was with Darryn she had absolutely no shame. Loving him the way she did, it was easy to give everything of herself to him. But wow, this...? She glanced at the story again. This was taking bold to a whole new level.

Well, she wanted to know if he still loved her, still wanted her. This was one way to find out.

She picked up her phone and scrolled to Darryn's number. Her finger hovered over his name. Inhaling deeply, she finally pressed it.

Chapter Eighteen

D ARRYN HAD HAD enough. This was a bloody waste of everyone's time. The meeting wasn't going as planned. This was supposed to be a mere formality so the papers could be signed, and now one of the sellers had all sorts of ridiculous stipulations.

They decided to build another hotel, somewhere along the Garden Route, a stretch of road along the southeastern coast of South Africa which extended from Mossel Bay in the Western Cape to the Storms River in the Eastern Cape. It was a popular tourist destination and included towns such as Knysna, Plettenberg Bay, and Nature's Valley, with George being the Garden Route's largest town and main administrative center.

They'd decided on the picturesque town of Knysna for their hotel. The piece of land they were interested in was near the Knysna Lagoon and would suit what they had in mind. Now all of a sudden, one of the owners was worried they'd put up something that wouldn't fit in with the environment. And this after Dale, the architect of the group, had spent weeks there before he'd drawn up plans for the hotel. But the guy kept finding fault.

Just as he opened his mouth, though, his phone rang. The caller ID indicated that Hannah was calling, and he promptly forgot what he was going to say.

Frowning, he got up and excused himself, in spite of Don's raised eyebrow. Hannah never phoned him, especially this time of day. He was usually the one who called and he hadn't spoken to her in a few days. A sense of urgency had him nearly running from the room. Something had to be wrong, very wrong.

"Hannah, what's wrong?"

"Hi, Darryn." She breathed in his ear. "Nothing is wrong. I...I was wondering..."

Silence.

"Yes?" he asked in a clipped voice, his heartbeat settling. She was obviously fine.

"What are you wearing?"

Stunned, he took the phone from his ear to make sure it was actually Hannah. What the hell?

"Hannah? I'm not sure what—"

"I'm wearing pearls and a smile," her voice whispered in his ear.

And his body reacted. Immediately.

"Damnit, Hannah, I'm in an important meeting! And you call me to tell me what you're wearing? Are you crazy?" He hissed, looking around if anyone was close by. He turned around so he could face the wall. How the hell was he supposed to walk back into the meeting now, looking like this?

"I'm—"

The next minute the line was down, and Darryn groaned out loud. The full impact of what had just happened only now dawned on him. If he wasn't mistaken, Hannah contacted him for some phone sex and he reacted like an absolute idiot.

He tried to call her back, but her phone didn't even ring, she had to have switched it off completely.

At that moment, the doors to the conference room opened, and the three sellers walked out, all clearly fed up. They briefly nodded in his direction before they headed for the elevators.

Dumbstruck, Darryn stared after them. The meeting couldn't be over already, damnit. They hadn't solved anything! He stormed back into the conference room where his three brothers were still sitting around the table.

"What the hell happened?" he asked.

"Well, if you were here, you would have known," Don said irritably while he got up and closed his laptop.

"The ball in is their court. They know they won't get another offer like ours for the land. They have until tomorrow to give us a final answer. There is an alternative piece of land we can try, but the plans I've been working on are based on this property. Damnit, what a bloody mess!" Dale growled.

"What call was so important that you had to leave?" David asked, obviously also irritated.

"It…it was Hannah," Darryn said, frustrated. So not only had the meeting been a waste of time, Hannah was also not talking to him.

"So, what was so important that you had to leave to take her call?" asked David.

"She phoned to…" he began before he realized there was no way he could tell his brother about the mess he'd just made with Hannah's call.

Don slapped his shoulder as he passed him. "As long as you weren't having phone sex while we were battling alone inside—"

"How the hell did you know that?" Darryn asked. Only when the words had popped out of his mouth, did he realize he'd said them out loud.

His brothers all stared at him.

"Oh, man!" David finally chuckled. "I hope it was worth it."

"At least someone had some fun this morning," Dale grumbled.

"I wasn't having fun, damnit! I thought she was in trouble and then—"

Now all three of his brothers were openly laughing at him.

"So, you've screwed up phone sex?" Dale snickered. "You really need help."

"I could give you some pointers," Don said with a poker face.

"Me too," David piped in.

"Get the hell off my back," Darryn snarled, walking toward the elevator. "I'll fix it myself."

As the elevator doors closed, he looked up to see his brothers still laughing. Bloody hell. He didn't even want to think what was going on in Hannah's mind at the moment. He had never been good with any kind of telephone conversation, never mind the sexy kind. Which, come to think of it, he'd never even considered up to now.

And, to be honest, he hadn't thought Hannah would be this adventurous. But then he remembered her as she was standing behind Stephen White—arms held high, ready to clobber him with the heel of her shoe.

Man, she was everything he'd ever wanted in a woman—so why the hell was he here in South Africa when she was New York?

HANNAH WISHED THERE was a hole she could crawl into and stay there. She was mortified. Of course, Darryn would be busy in the middle of the day. What was she thinking calling him without checking what time it was and telling him what she wasn't wearing? It hadn't even occurred to her to look at the time, to think about what he might be doing.

But, hell, he could have been nicer about it!

If he was in love with her as he'd said… That was obviously the problem. Over the past two weeks, he hadn't mentioned loving her once. Yes, he had phoned and they'd talked, if the one-word sentences she got out of him could be described as talking.

This whole thing was messing with her head, and she should be concentrating on what she was doing.

"Hannah, sweetheart, please focus," the photographer said, his smile much stiffer than it had been earlier that morning.

She tried to clear her head. The shoot had been scheduled for that morning, and it was now already way past lunch. It was her fault entirely. The photographer was being very patient with her. She was a professional; she should be doing her job, not thinking about Darryn.

And for the next hour she managed to clear her head, kept her focus on what she was supposed to be doing. When they were done, she walked over to the photographer and apologized for being distracted.

"Don't sweat it," he said, much happier now that they were finished. "Man trouble?" he asked with a grin.

Hannah shook her head, fed up with herself. Darryn was interfering with her life, with her work. This kind of thing had never happened to her before. The last thing she wanted was to have a reputation as someone who behaved unprofessionally.

As much as she didn't want to believe it, it was now obvious to her that Darryn's feelings had changed. It was time she moved on with her life.

AT ELEVEN O'CLOCK, Hannah crawled into bed, too tired to even bother switching off the light. They rehearsed the whole afternoon and then she had a personal trainer come over for a gym session. Now she was bone tired and fervently hoped she would be able to fall asleep. She had a day to herself tomorrow and wouldn't have to worry about getting up early.

Her phone rang. Her eyes closed, she felt on her bedside table until her fingers found it. It was probably her agent.

"Hi," she said, answering without checking who was calling.

"Still wearing only that smile and pearls?" Darryn asked huskily in her ear.

Her eyes flew open. "Darryn?"

"Or are you wearing that sexy red lace thing you sometimes wear to bed. The one that leaves those long, sexy legs of yours bare so my hands can slowly stroke…"

Wide awake now and ticked off, Hannah sat upright, pushing her hair back. "I'm trying to sleep, Darryn, good night." She ended the call.

She'd brazenly tried to talk sexily to him last night, but he hadn't been interested. Now, after she'd been suffering from humiliation for a whole day, and she was finally tired enough to go to sleep, he wanted to say sexy things to her and she was supposed to be happy about it? Aaargghh!

She looked down at herself. It so happened that she was indeed wearing the damn red lace thing Darryn mentioned. And, to make matters worse, the delicious chills that went through her body while he was talking to her hadn't stopped yet. Irritated with herself, she stood up. She wasn't going to go back to sleep right now, so she might as well have a cup of tea.

Not bothering to put on anything over her nighty, she walked to the kitchen. The intercom beeped as she put out a hand to switch on the light. Who would be visiting this time of night? It could be a courier, although they usually deliver stuff to the security guard downstairs.

She pressed the button. "Yes?" she said.

"It's me." The voice sounded remarkably like Darryn's.

What was going on?

"Hannah? I'm sorry about yesterday. I'm sorry I acted like an idiot, but I'm here, in New York and I…I have to see you. Please let me in?"

She pressed the button to let him enter the building and stood staring at the door, her breath lodged somewhere in the back of her throat. Was she dreaming? Had everything that had happened over the last two years finally caught up with her and she'd lost it completely? Because she could swear Darryn was on his way up to her apartment.

A loud knock propelled her forward and she flung open

the door. And there he was, gorgeous and sexy and—she put out a hand to touch his face—and real.

His eyes were bloodshot, his hair standing on end, but it was Darryn. His gaze slowly traveled over her, igniting flames just below the surface of her skin so that when he finally dropped his suitcase and opened his arms, she was ready to burst into flames. With a cry, she walked into his embrace.

Chapter Nineteen

H E HAD BEEN ready to grovel, but before he could utter a word, his arms were full of woman, his senses steeped in her scent, his mouth captured by her soft, urgent lips. An apology would have to wait.

Kicking the door shut behind him, he lifted Hannah into his arms without taking his mouth from hers.

He had never been to her New York apartment, but he had noticed the sitting room on the right, so the bedroom had to be on the left. Somewhere.

"Last door," she said against his lips, and he got there in two long strides.

He lowered her onto the bed and stood back, just staring at her. In most of his dreams she had been wearing this little red number. Smiling, she leaned back on her elbows.

Without taking his eyes off of her, he unbuckled his belt, lifted his shirt over his head, and tried to push the zipper of his pants down. "I was going to go slow," he said through clenched teeth, struggling with the zipper, "but I haven't been with you for two damn weeks."

Swearing, he yanked on the zipper until it finally gave

way and he could kick his pants to the side. When he looked up, Hannah was staring up at him, now wearing only that smile she'd spoken about yesterday.

He was a dead man. That was his last coherent thought as he moved over her.

HANNAH DROWNED IN Darryn's hot gaze as he hoisted himself above her. His eyes raked feverishly over her. She had been dreaming about being with him like this for the last two weeks. But she hadn't realized how quickly one look from him could make her lose control.

She was burning for him, light-headed with need. Unashamedly, her body lifted upward, urging him to hurry. But his lips only teased hers, not claiming hers like they had minutes ago. With a grunt, her arms and legs snaked around him, pulling him closer so he would have to stop torturing her and kiss her.

Fusing her mouth with his, she held him tightly. Every centimeter of her skin was plastered against his. She was amazed at how perfectly the upper part of his body fit around her curves, as if their bodies had been designed precisely for one another.

HE DESPERATELY TRIED to remember that he was supposed to be civilized, but he was losing control. Her scent infiltrated every cell of his body, heated his blood until it raced through his veins and thundered in his ears.

Her back arched and he let go. Folding her long tresses around his one hand, he moved her head so he could get to her throat, to the soft spot just below her ear.

She gasped; he pushed her back so his hands and mouth could move over her damp skin. Frantically, he savored and caressed, but he had to get more of her, needed more of her.

His mouth moved farther down over her heated flesh, possessed her breasts.

It was impossible to breathe. The air around them was too thick. Flames were licking just below the surface of his skin, overheating his entire system. She was as desperate to touch him, to taste him, her hands clutching and unclutching his shoulders.

His hand found her wet and ready for him. He lifted his head to watch her. Her eyes were closed, her face aglow with pleasure. Shuddering, he stroked her body. He craved her, he needed her, *now.*

His muscles quivered as he hoisted himself above her. She opened her eyes; they were wild with passion, dark with want. She whispered his name over and over again.

Blind with need, he pushed into her and she clamped around him. He was finally where he wanted, needed to be. With her, in her, a part of her. He was home.

SHE WAS BURNING, burning, burning. Passion had blurred her vision and she couldn't see anything. There was only Darryn—his breath in her ear, his hands on her body as he took them up and up to a height she'd never reached before. There she clung to the moment until he trembled above her. With her name a mantra on his lips, the tempest finally swept them away to a point where time and place had no meaning.

When Hannah opened her eyes, she stared into Darryn's. She was lying on her side, her hands tucked under her face. He was lying on his elbow, staring down at her.

She put out a hand and touched his face again. "You're really here."

He smiled and bent down to kiss her. "I'm here," he said, trailing a hand lazily up and down her side. "I behaved like an idiot when you called. We were in a meeting, and I was ready to punch this one guy…"

She winced. "And I phoned wanting phone sex! I still can't believe I did that," she said, her face in the palm of her hand.

"Hey," Darryn said, taking her hand away. "I love it that you're not too shy to show me what you feel." He smiled and wiggled his eyebrows. "Next time you phone, asking me what I'm wearing, I'll tell you."

A blush crept up her neck. "I've never done anything like that before," she said. "But with you…I become a brazen hussy!" she cried out and pressed her face in the pillow.

His hand stopped stroking her side and cupped her breast. "Any schoolboy's fantasy." He chuckled and kissed the top of her shoulder. "I love you," he whispered, kissing her back. "And I love what you do to me." His words disappeared on her skin.

Hannah sighed and turned on her back. Her arms slid around his neck. "I love you too," she whispered. "I hate being away from you," she said and kissed him.

He stilled.

"What?" she asked.

"Your modeling career…I've been thinking. It's your work that's keeping us apart," he said.

Hannah could actually feel her blood cooling. "So, you think my work is the problem?"

"Well, yes. If you're not working, you can be with me and we can travel together when I have to be somewhere. What do you think?"

"What do I think?" she asked softly.

Before he could answer, though, she shoved him away and scooted off the bed. Grabbing the sheet, she quickly folded it around her body, her hands shaking.

"What?" Darryn asked, totally bewildered.

Grinding her teeth, she rounded on him. "What do I think?" she repeated. "Thank you for realizing that I actually do think—really big of you. I love you, but you are behaving like a complete jerk. What made you think that I would leave my job to be at your beck and call?"

"Because we'll be together?" he said, clearly dumbstruck that she hadn't jumped at the chance to leave everything behind her at the drop of a hat.

"Together? And for how long? Until you've had enough of me, until you discover I'm not what you thought I was? How long did you have in mind?"

He slipped off the bed and pulled on his pants. "Hannah, I don't know, okay? I don't have everything figured out, but I mistakenly thought because you love me, you'd be happy to stay with me!"

"Come to think of it, your job is also keeping us apart. If you're not working you can stay with me, go with me when I travel. How does that sound?" she asked coolly.

⭐

DARRYN STARED AT Hannah, not quite sure he'd heard her correctly. But the tilt of her chin and the battle in her eyes confirmed her words.

"I...I..." He didn't know what to say. He closed his mouth. This was not how he thought this conversation would go. "You're being unreasonable. I'm leaving," he said, buttoning up his shirt.

Her eyes blazed but she inhaled deeply. "Of course you're leaving," Hannah said and turning her back on him, walked regally toward the bathroom. "You are not getting what you want. I don't want to heel when you want me to. I'm the one being unreasonable, so why would you stay?"

Just before she closed the door, the sheet slipped, giving him a last glance of a sexy thigh.

And of course, his body reacted immediately to the sight.

"Damnit, that's not what I said!" he shouted after her.

But the bathroom door remained closed. Undecided, he looked around him. Why the hell was she so difficult? He was part of a business; what a ridiculous notion to think he'd quit his job. Of course he couldn't simply walk away.

Staying here for the moment was not going to accomplish anything. He'd give her a day to think about what he'd said, and then he'd try to talk to her again.

HANNAH LISTENED WITH her ear against the door. After a few moments, the sound of footsteps down the short corridor reached her. It was silent for a few minutes before the front door was opened and closed.

She felt like crying, but she was so angry she could throw something. Her job was keeping them apart? And when she'd turned the tables on him and asked him to leave his job, she was being unreasonable?

Tears threatened to escape, but she wiped her eyes crossly. Crying was not going to solve anything—it left her with swollen eyes and a blocked nose and the problem still unsolved.

She opened the bathroom door and walked back into her room. Her gaze fell on the unmade bed and she turned away quickly. Grabbing her laptop, she stormed out of her room. Coffee. She needed coffee, and then she had to talk to her sisters.

Glancing at her watch, she sent a text to Caitlin. She needed man advice urgently, she didn't care what time it was. Her sisters and Dana would have to figure out quickly how they could all get to one place so that they could Skype.

Chapter Twenty

H ER TWO SISTERS' and Dana's faces stared at her from the screen of her laptop. She had just told them about Darryn's idea that she should quit her job.

Dana leaned forward. "And he didn't say anything about getting married?"

Hannah sighed, not so sure anymore that talking to her family would help. "Nobody is talking about getting married," she said irritably. She had been wondering the same freaking thing.

"But he wants you to quit your job and move in with him?" Caitlin asked.

"Stay with him, was how he put it," Hannah said.

"And you don't want to?" Zoe asked.

"Want to what?"

"Stay with him."

Hannah rubbed her face. "Yes, I want to be with him, but not if he has this ultimatum—leave your job or else."

"But is that what he said?" asked Zoe.

Hannah frowned. "No, but that's what he implied," Hannah said indignantly. "My work is the problem; I have to quit my job. You should have seen his face when I suggested he stopped working and stay with me."

Caitlin smiled. "Hannah, sweetie, let's begin at the beginning. Darryn is a man. And a man is…" she motioned with her hands.

"A man?" Dana giggled.

"Yes," Caitlin said, nodding her head. "They know what they want, they have long conversations about things with themselves, and by the time they talk to you, they only mention the tail end of that whole conversation. The result usually is that what they say and what they mean are two completely different things."

Dana and Zoe nodded in agreement.

"He was very clear with what he wanted," Hannah grumbled. "My job is what is keeping us apart, and that has to change."

Caitlin cocked her head. "So you don't have a problem being away from him for long periods of time?"

"That's not what I said!" Hannah cried in frustration. "But why do I have to make all the sacrifices?"

"Well, if you feel that being with Darryn means you'll have to sacrifice something, you shouldn't do it. He is obviously not the right one for you then, because I can tell you, for the right man, you'd give up everything in a heartbeat," Zoe said and shrugged. "A pity, I thought you two are a cute couple."

"It's not that I don't want to give up everything for him,

it's…" Hannah began hotly but realized she didn't know how to finish the sentence. It was only what?

"And if he asks you to marry him, will that change what you are willing to give up?" Zoe asked. "Is that your ultimatum?"

"It's not an ultimatum, but—"

Before Hannah could continue, though, Caitlin looked over her shoulder to something behind her. "We have to go, Hannah. You and I have talked about this. You are the only one who can decide what to do, what will be right for you. The question you have to answer for yourself is this—will you be happy being away from Darryn?"

And with waves and smiles, they ended the call.

Hannah sat staring at the blank screen. She had hoped to get some sympathy from her sisters—they were all twenty-first century women, for goodness sake! But she was obviously mistaken. But then they all still worked. Nobody had asked them to quit their work.

Granted, Caitlin moved her rooms to her home with Don; Zoe still had her interior design business, although she did most of her work for the hotels now; and Dana was still teaching although she had to move to Cape Town.

They all had to adjust.

Hannah stood up slowly. They all had to adjust. Did the men, though? No, the damn men… Her thoughts trailed off. They also had to adjust, she grudgingly acknowledged. Don wasn't cycling competitively anymore, not because Caitlin asked him not to, but because he wanted to have more time with his family.

The same was true of Dale and David. Their previous lives as footloose bachelors came to a screeching halt once they'd met their wives. But they didn't look unhappy—on the contrary.

Was the reason she was so angry because Darryn asked her to quit her job or because he hadn't asked her to marry him? Would she have reacted differently if he'd given her a ring? Why?

A ring on her finger and a signature on a piece of paper didn't make that much difference. Somewhere along the way, he'd be tired of her and would leave, whether or not they were married. That was what her dad did.

But Darryn wasn't her dad. She remembered his eyes. On her. Like Caitlin said—the Cavallo men only had eyes for their loved ones.

Hannah groaned out loud. What did it all mean? Her brain refused to work, she was so tired. She walked back to her room and crawled under the sheets. Darryn's scent was still hanging in the room, was still lingering on the sheets. She pressed her face into it and with his name on her lips, drifted off.

She'd think again tomorrow.

DARRYN THREW THE hotel room key on the small table near

the door and looked around him. He didn't want to be here. But how did he get Hannah to listen to him? After he'd left Hannah, he'd gotten a hotel room and had then walked around the city, trying to figure out what to do.

That had been a few hours ago, and he still didn't know what he should do. Why was she being so difficult? She said she loved him, but she didn't want to be with him? How was that supposed to work?

His phone rang, and he quickly picked it up.

But it was his brother Don, not Hannah as he'd hoped.

"Well, at least you had the brains to go to Hannah, but it sounds as if you made a mess of the rest!" Don exclaimed over the phone.

Darryn swore. "What the hell do you know about it?"

"Women talk."

Darryn grimaced. "So I'm the bad guy without giving my side of the story? I really don't need this from you now. I—"

"Why did you go to New York?" Don interrupted him.

"To be with Hannah, of course."

"And?"

"And to ask her to quit her job so we could be together. That's what you guys did, right? I'd thought that would be what she wanted as well, but obviously—"

"What exactly does this 'be together' mean?" asked Don.

"That we'd get married, stay in the same house, in the same place, I assumed but—"

"And did you ask her to marry you?"

Darryn did a double take. Married to Hannah. He hadn't thought about it, but he liked the sound of it.

"No, I didn't ask in so many words, but isn't that what being together means?"

Don laughed. "Man, you have a lot to learn, and clearly you haven't learned anything from the mistakes Dale and David made. When I gave them a few pointers, you fled, if memory serves me right. I was the only one who knew what to do," he said, sounding pleased with himself. "Let me give you a tip. You have to tell a woman exactly what you mean, what you want. I know, we don't understand that. But you can either love a woman or understand her. I know what I prefer."

"So if I ask her to marry me, she'll quit her job?"

"You don't tell a Sutherland woman what to do. Haven't you learned anything? Get a ring, go down on one knee, ask her in so many words to marry you—the whole shebang. As for the rest? You ask, you suggest, you compromise, you never, ever tell her."

Darryn swore.

"If you love her, you do whatever it takes. It's that simple."

Long after Don had ended the call, Darryn still stood with the phone in his hand.

His phone rang again, and he grimaced when he saw the caller ID. So someone had spoken to his mother as well.

Bloody hell.

"Mom," he said in a clipped voice.

"Wow, you sound chirpy," she said.

"I know why you're calling."

"You do?"

"Yeah. You heard that I haven't asked Hannah to marry me already, and now you're phoning to tell me what I should and shouldn't do. I'm all grown up, damnit!"

"I haven't spoken to any of your brothers today, but thank you for telling me how stupid you've been. You love the woman; what is the problem? Don't you want to marry her?"

Darryn bit off a swear word. "Yes, I want to marry her, but she doesn't want to quit her job!"

"Please tell me you didn't ask her to do that?"

Darryn swore. "It's much more complicated than that, Mom," Darryn said, wishing he'd never taken the damn call. "What about her career? She became angry when I suggested she quit her job. She asked if I would quit mine. What would I do? It's a bloody mess!"

"Life is complicated and messy, Darryn. Surely you know that by now? As a couple, you give and take. You're spoiled. Just because you and your brothers are owners of hotels and have money doesn't mean things will always work out as planned. And you definitely won't always get your way."

"I know that!" he called out, frustrated.

"Any woman who can use her high heel as a weapon

when she has to is someone to fight for, in my book."

"I know that too."

"Marriage, my dear boy, is a partnership. You compromise, you talk, you give, and you balance. Your dad knew I loved cooking and, as soon as he could, he helped me to start Rosa's, even if it meant our whole lives moved to the restaurant. It's not always easy, but the upside is priceless."

"Yeah? And what is that?"

"You get to love one another." And with those words, she ended the call.

Darryn stared at the phone for long minutes, images of Hannah flitting through his mind—Hannah on the beach, her toned body moving to his silent requests. Hannah in his bed, her hair sprayed out over his pillow. Hannah standing up to Stephen White, her shoe high above her head, ready to defend herself. Hannah loving him with abandon, pleasure lighting up her face.

And then those messy pieces in his mind that had fallen into place two years ago when he'd seen Hannah for the first time, moved, shifted and settled again, this time creating a clearer picture—of him and Hannah, together. And somewhere in the background a couple of kids were chasing a Labrador, kids with their mother's blue eyes and blonde hair.

None of the questions that had been bothering him earlier seemed to be problems any longer. They had to find a way to make it work, because... He grinned.

Like Don had said, it really was that simple. He loved her; he wanted to be with her. *Whatever it takes.*

Chapter Twenty-One

HANNAH STOOD IN front of the big windows of her apartment, looking out over New York. She'd actually slept through the morning and felt more relaxed. She hadn't heard a word from Darryn since he'd left early that morning. He might have left for South Africa, although she hoped not.

But, ever since she'd woken up, things were clearer, somehow. Darryn loved her. He'd told her in so many words, but more than that, he'd shown her. Yes, in the grand gesture to fly to Paris when he thought she was in trouble, flying to New York to be with her, but also in all the small gestures—the way he put a hand on the small of her back when they crossed a street, the way he opened doors for her, the way he watched her, the way he made love to her.

She didn't know why he hadn't asked her to marry him, but she knew he loved her. A piece of paper was not going to change the way she felt. A sigh escaped. But, yes, if he asked her, she would say yes. No wait, she would yell out that yes!

And she knew now that for him she would give up everything—her modeling, her apartments, her life. In a heartbeat. She had to find a way to tell him that.

A loud knock on her front had her turning around. Dazed, she stared at the front door. It had to be Darryn. She moved forward.

He hadn't left. They had another chance to make this right. She ran the last few steps and flung open the door.

And there he was—tall, gorgeous, and smiling uncertainly.

"Yes," she said very calmly, while clutching the door frame for support. "Of course, I'll bloody well marry you!"

DARRYN WAS STILL thinking how exactly to do what he wanted to do when the door opened. He was probably still suffering from jet lag, because he could have sworn the exquisite creature in front of him had just accepted a marriage proposal he had yet to make.

But before he could say anything, she was in his arms, and talking became unimportant.

Scooping her up, he closed his mouth over hers and walked toward her room with long strides. At times like this, talking was overrated. He could show her more convincingly how he felt by simply loving her.

SHE WAS LYING on top of a warm, hard body. A hand was stroking her back, up and down, up and down. For the first time in three weeks, she felt at peace. Darryn was with her.

Hannah opened her eyes and turned her head.

They had to talk, she knew that. She'd accepted a marriage proposal and hadn't even been asked!

That was taking being brazen and bold to a whole new level. A blush crept up her neck, and she buried her face in Darryn's body.

Beneath her, his body started shaking, and it took her a few seconds to realize the rumbling beneath her ear was his laughter.

She looked up and scowled. "Why are you laughing?"

"You're blushing," he teased and combed his fingers through her hair. "And that after last night and just now!"

There was no way she could stop the smile. "We made love. I could never be embarrassed about that, although I never thought I'd be so…"

"Innovative? Creative? Sexy? Amazing?" he said pulling her up so their eyes were on the same level.

"So were you," she breathed and kissed him.

"So, what are you embarrassed about?" he said, still with that lazy smile.

"I…" She buried her face in his neck. "I said…no, make that I *yelled* that I'll marry you, and you hadn't even asked. So, please, can we just forget about my outburst? You don't have to ask me to…"

He stilled and warily she lifted her face. "What did you just say?" he asked.

She rolled away from him, but before she could get off

the bed, she was pulled backward and was lying on her back, pinned down by his leg.

"What did you say?" he asked again, his voice cool.

Sighing, she rubbed her face. "Just forget about what I said. I was at the end of a long argument with myself. Can we please move on and forget—"

He put a finger on her lips so she had to stop speaking.

"I don't talk much," he said. "But I try to show you how I feel. Why do you think I caught a twenty-one hour commercial flight to New York? Merely for the sex?"

All the oxygen left her body in one swoosh. She stared at him, trying to read his face, trying to make sense of his words. "What do you mean?"

"Hell, I can't screw this up again. Why is it so damn hard?" he muttered.

With a string of swear words, he scooted off the bed. She sat up, staring at Darryn's back. Buck naked and mouth-wateringly sexy, he looked around, picked up his pants, patted the pockets, and took something out before he turned back to her.

She kept her eyes on his face. She needed to breathe, but she didn't want to move. With two long strides, he reached the bed again. With his gorgeous naked body right in front of her, it took all of her willpower to keep her eyes above his neck, but she wanted to make sure she saw every emotion, every expression.

Something was about to happen, something she had

thought was impossible.

"I have this long list of dos and don'ts I got from the mothers, and I was going to take you out to dinner, go down on my knee, and the whole damn thing, but now you…and I…" He motioned with his hand toward her.

At this point, her eyes simply refused to stay on his face. She still wasn't quite sure what he was trying to say, but there were other parts of his body that had no trouble communicating. A giggle threatened to escape, but she swallowed it forcefully. This was so not the time to become hysterical.

With a tremendous effort, she forced her eyes upward again. The expression on his face was priceless.

"I'm trying to ask you to marry me, damnit, and you're not paying attention!" he said, and he dropped his hand holding the little box.

For a few seconds more, she was so busy trying to keep her eyes on his face, she didn't grasp the meaning of his words. But then…there it was, the flicker of vulnerability. And finally, she understood.

She tried to breathe. Inhaling was supposed to be instinctive, not something one had a problem with, but there was a huge lump in her throat that refused to let any air into her body.

Light-headed, overjoyed, and crying, she jumped up on the bed and threw herself into Darryn's arms. He staggered backward, his arms folding around her.

"Why are you crying? What have I done wrong now?" he cried out, frantically pushing her hair back from her face.

"Because..." She hiccupped, "I'm happy!" she said and kissed him all over his face.

"Oh." He sighed, obviously relieved. "I've heard about that." He pushed her back on the bed. "Sit over there, I'm not done yet," he said and looked around again.

"What are you looking for now?" she asked, wiping her eyes.

"I...can't talk to you if you look like this," he said through clenched teeth and, grabbing a corner of the sheet, he draped it over her body.

Smiling, she crossed her arms over it. Her heart was beating frantically, her mouth was dry, and she wished she could have recorded all of this. But looking up into his face she realized—that wasn't necessary. She would never forget this day, this moment, here with Darryn.

DARRYN STARED DOWN at Hannah's lovely face. He knew the answer to his question already. She had said yes hours earlier.

But, within seconds, she was going to put his ring on her finger, and then she would be his fiancé—he never even thought he'd wanted one of those. But standing here, with absolutely no clothes on, he had literally and figuratively nothing more to hide behind—he'd run out of excuses to be with her a long time ago. He wanted this, yes, but much more than that, he needed this, needed her. His heart had surrendered to her over two years ago already.

He sank down on his knees at the side of the bed and opened the little box.

"Hannah Sutherland, you stole my heart two years ago on a beach on Mahé, and I've never been able to get it back. Now, I don't want it back. Ever. I love you with every fiber of my being, with every breath I take. And I know this is going to be crazy. You work long hours in various cities around the world and so do I. I'll figure out the logistics if I know you're by my side."

He inhaled deeply and took her hand in his. "Will you marry me and be my wife?" he asked and held the little box out to her. "That's it. There are no other stipulations. You don't have to quit your job; we'll figure something out. Hell, if need be, I'll quit mine. Exactly how this will work, I don't know yet, but I do know I never want to be without you again."

She stared down at the ring for long minutes. Oh, hell. Maybe he should have waited and asked his mother or one of his sisters-in-law about the ring.

He opened his mouth to tell her they could exchange it, but she sniffled, wiped her cheeks, and took the ring out of the box with great care.

Again, she stared at it without saying anything.

"If you don't like it, we can exchange it, but I

thought…"

She lifted her eyes up—emotion had darkened her blue eyes. "It's exquisite," she whispered.

"The blue of the sapphires reminded me of the color of your eyes when we make love," he whispered and took the ring from her.

Gently, he pushed it over her finger, praying it would fit. It slid easily over her long finger—it was a perfect fit.

She stared at it, tears streaming down her face. "What's with the damn tears?" he finally asked and lifted her onto his lap. He never could stand a woman crying.

She put an arm around his neck. "We Sutherland women cry when we're happy, and I'm so, so happy." She smiled through the tears and held up her hand. "It's perfect."

"Look, it's very plain, but I didn't think you'd like an ostentatious ring. But if you want something more—"

"You've been paying attention," she smiled. "I don't like flashy jewelry."

"I know," he said. "But if you want a different ring…"

She put a finger on his mouth. "I love it," she smiled. "Let me show you something." She bent forward and picked up her phone. "I've never been one of those girls who started planning her wedding even before she could walk, but when Caitlin got married, she started this wedding board on Pinterest and she pinned all things wedding," she said while scrolling down her phone. "And then Zoe and Dana got married and made boards."

"Boards?" Darryn asked, not quite following her.

"Yes, on Pinterest. Anyway, then I…" She smiled self-consciously while still scrolling. "Well, I've been thinking about weddings and dresses and rings and on the flight over, I found myself creating my own board."

She clicked on her phone and a picture opened up. Wordlessly, she handed him the phone. It was a picture of a wedding ring—almost the exact ring he had just given her.

He stared down at his ring on her finger and was amazed to realize his throat was clogged up.

"Darryn?" she said.

He had to swallow hard before he looked at her. Her soft smile told him exactly how moved she was.

"I've told you already," she said. "But I'll gladly answer you again." She folded both arms around his neck and pulled his face closer. "Somehow, you get me. You see beyond the model and know me, love me. You knew exactly the kind of ring I'd like. So, yes, of course I'll marry you," she whispered. "I love you. And you don't have to quit your job. We'll figure something out."

The smile that nearly split his face in two started deep within him.

"Yes." He breathed, and gathering her close, he fell back on the bed taking her with him.

Laughing, she held him tightly. "Can we please make love now? It's either that or you have to put on your clothes. There is no way I can look at you one second longer and not jump your bones." She giggled before she started kissing him.

He threw his arms out on the bed and laughed "By all means—jump my bones!"

And with great enthusiasm she did exactly that.

Chapter Twenty-Two

"OH, THAT IS *soooo* romantic." Her mother sighed and leaned back against the chair.

"Our Darryn tends to be very spontaneous when he feels deeply about something, and he obviously feels deeply about you," Rosa said with bright eyes. "Jumping on a plane to be with you—that's Darryn." She smiled. "He wasn't sure about the details, but he knew what he wanted."

Hannah smiled. She and Darryn had called everybody from New York to announce their engagement. They returned yesterday, and this morning she opened her eyes to a message from her mother, informing her everyone was coming over for a glass of champagne and a chat. Everyone, of course, included her sisters, Darryn's mother, and her mother.

Darryn's brothers and dad had taken him away, "to give him some pointers about women," as they'd put it. Her sisters had been grilling her about the details of the proposal.

"Now your story is really only beginning," her mother said with a smile, blissfully happy to have heard a real-life love story playing out around her.

"So, come, on, give us some details. Did he take to you a restaurant? What were you wearing when he proposed? How did he ask? Come on, give. We're old married women," Dana said.

Hannah felt the blush creeping up her neck again. "Well, it...I...we..."

"Don't you remember?" teased Zoe.

"Of course I do. It's just..." She glanced at her future mother-in-law who was cooking in the kitchen. Well, she'd hear about it at some point. She might as well tell the whole story.

"We never left the apartment," she said, and her sisters leaned forward.

"Yes?" Caitlin breathed.

"In fact, we never even left the bedroom." She paused for effect. "Or the bed, for that matter."

"So you were on your bed and wearing..." Dana asked.

"Absolutely nothing," Hannah declared with a straight face.

THE FEMININE GIGGLES welcomed them home.

Darryn opened his front door and motioned his brothers and dad inside. His mother had to be cooking, because delicious smells welcomed them.

"This has to be the shortest bachelor's party in history," Dale grumbled.

"Oh, no," Don said, slapping him on the back. "He's not getting off that easily. We'll get him at a time he's not in such a hurry to return to Hannah."

"Well, then you'll have a long wait," Darryn said, moving toward the voices in his living room.

He rounded the corner, searched the faces until he found her. His heart settled; his shoulders relaxed. With long strides, he made his way over to her.

"There you are," he said and lifted her from the couch for a kiss.

"Now that," her mother exclaimed behind him, "that's the stuff romance stories are made of!"

A MONTH LATER, he was standing on the beach in Mahé where he'd seen Hannah for the first time, waiting for his bride to appear. They both wanted the wedding to be held there. Standing with the ocean behind him, flanked by his brothers, he felt ten feet tall.

Today, he was marrying his Hannah. She still had contracts she couldn't break, he had work that had to be done, but they were figuring things out as they went along. Whenever he could, he traveled with her, and so far they hadn't spent a night apart.

They had both agreed on a family-only wedding. The whole ceremony had been kept quiet—a circus was the last thing they wanted.

His mother, Hannah's mother, and his sisters-in-law nearly had a fit when he'd grudgingly agreed to wait a month to marry Hannah. It was impossible, they said, nobody could do that, they moaned, but in spite of all their complaints, they managed to pull it off.

There was movement on the beach. His heart tripped. And then Hannah's sisters and Dana came walking down a pathway of pink rose petals, but he barely even glanced at them.

His eyes searched for Hannah. And there she was. This time his heart stopped completely. Smiling, her hand on her mother's arm, Hannah glided toward him. A smile started deep within him. She was wearing a beautiful white dress with a skirt made of layers and layers of white tulle.

As he stared, she stopped, lifted the layers and, laughingly, she twirled. With a swoosh, the oxygen returned to his body, and his feet were moving before he knew what he was doing.

"LOOK AT HIM, sweetheart, he can't wait, he's coming for you," her mother said while they were only halfway down the aisle. "This, I'm going to remember." She chuckled and leaned in for a kiss.

Hannah looked up and there he was—his brown eyes nearly pitch-black with emotion, not wavering from her face.

"I'll look after her, always," he said gruffly to her mother and kissed her.

As if walking on air, she put her hand on his arm and together they moved forward to where the minister was waiting for them, an indulgent smile on his face.

And with the sound of the sea in her ears, the faces of their family close by, she and Darryn promised one another a lifetime of loving. All the questions and the what ifs were forgotten. With Darryn by her side, she was ready for any challenge.

"WILL YOU WAIT here for two minutes?" Darryn asked and slid her down his body so she could stand. "Two minutes," he said and went into his room. Their room now.

Hannah hugged herself. They'd spent the most amazing week on Mahé and had only arrived in Cape Town earlier tonight. Darryn had been quiet on the way here. She now knew him well enough to know he was probably planning another surprise.

"Okay, Mrs. Calvallo," he interrupted her thoughts and picked her up. "Let's do this properly."

Giggling, she threw her arms around his neck as he walked into the big room. And then she saw it. Slipping from his arms, she walked closer. Above the bed, hung a huge print of her, twirling around in the pink tulle skirt. He had to have taken this on the beach two years ago, that first time she'd seen him.

"Darryn," she whispered and felt his arms around her from behind. "That was the day…"

"I fell in love with you," they said simultaneously.

"That," he said and pointed toward the picture, "was the moment you looked up and saw me. And that was the moment you touched my very being. And that was the moment my heart ultimately surrendered to you. How could I not fall for you?"

He pulled her into his arms.

The End

If you enjoyed this book, please leave a review at your favorite online retailer!
Even if it's just a sentence or two it makes all the difference.

Thanks for reading *The Ultimate Surrender* by Elsa Winckler!

Discover your next romance at TulePublishing.com.

TULE
PUBLISHING

If you enjoyed *The Ultimate Surrender*, you'll love the next book in....

The Cavallo Brothers series

Book 1: *An Impossible Attraction*

Book 2: *An Irresistible Temptation*

Book 3: *The Ultimate Surrender*

Available now at your favorite online retailer!

About the Author

I have been reading love stories for as long as I can remember and when I 'met' the classic authors like Jane Austen, Elizabeth Gaskell, Henry James The Brontë sisters, etc. during my Honours studies, I was hooked for life.

I married my college boyfriend and soul mate and after 43 years, 3 interesting and wonderful children and 3 beautiful grandchildren, he still makes me weak in the knees. We are fortunate to live in the picturesque little seaside village of Betty's Bay, South Africa with the ocean a block away and a beautiful mountain right behind us. And although life so far has not always been an easy ride, it has always been an exiting and interesting one!

I like the heroines in my stories to be beautiful, feisty, independent and headstrong. And the heroes must be strong but possess a generous amount of sensitivity. They are of course, also gorgeous! My stories typically incorporate the family background of the characters to better understand where they come from and who they are when we meet them in the story.

Thank you for reading

The Ultimate Surrender

If you enjoyed this book, you can find more from all our great authors at TulePublishing.com, or from your favorite online retailer.

TULE
PUBLISHING

Made in the USA
Coppell, TX
13 June 2023

18033152R00125